Class No. $\underline{\text{J}}$ Acc No. $\underline{\text{O/83080}}$

Author: $\underline{\text{Scott, M.}}$ Loc: $\underline{\text{14 AUG 1999}}$

LEABHARLANN
CHONDAE AN CHABHAIN

1. This book may b... ...returned on / befo... ...pe
2. A fine of 20p will ...or part of week a boo...

D0767368

	11 JAN 2003	

Reprinted 1992
First published 1991 by
WOLFHOUND PRESS
68 Mountjoy Square
Dublin 1

Wolfhound Press receives financial assistance from The Arts Council/ An Chomhairle Ealaíon, Dublin, Ireland.

British Library Cataloguing in Publication Data
Scott, Michael, *1959*—
    Wind lord
    I. Title
    823.914 [J]

    ISBN 0-86327-296-7

This book is fiction. All characters, incidents and names have no connection with any persons living or dead. Any apparent resemblence is purely coincidental.

For Lee, who wanted to know more about the bard.

Cover design and illustration: Peter Haigh
Map: Aileen Caffrey
Typesetting: Wolfhound Press
Printed by Cox & Wyman Ltd., Reading, Berkshire.

Contents

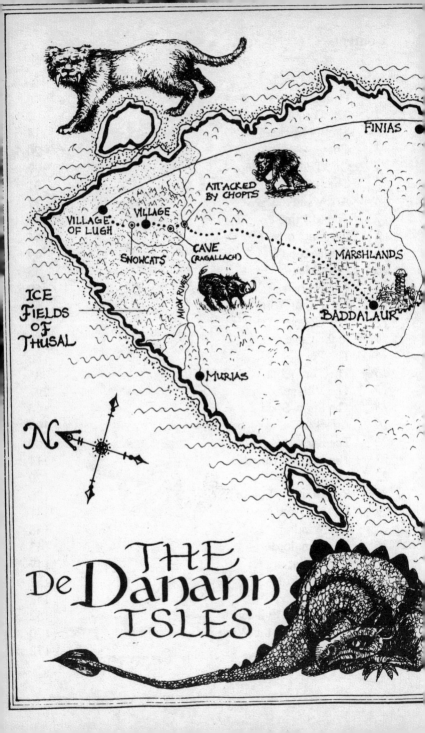

THE
De Danann
ISLES

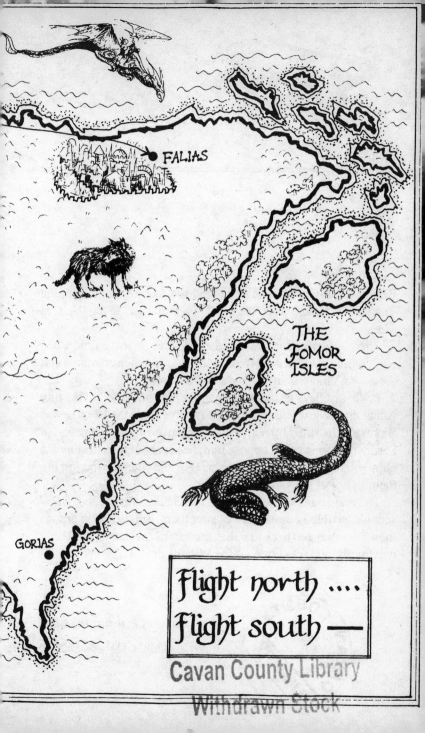

FALIAS

THE FOMOR ISLES

GORIAS

Flight north ....
Flight south —

Prologue

Before the Flood rose and changed the face of our world, the Tuatha De Danann ruled the vast De Danann Isle in the Western Ocean.

There was magic in the world at this time. It was a time when humans and non-humans lived side-by-side, when creatures that are now no more than myth walked the earth.

In the last days of the De Danann, before they fled to the tiny island that is now Erin, a mighty Emperor ruled the Isle. He was Balor, and he ruled by fear. He was a powerful magician, and to ensure that none could oppose him, he set about imprisoning the numerous wizards and sorcerers, mages and witches, and forcing them to reveal their magic.

The magicians scattered across the De Danann Isle, but Balor sent his terrible Fomor warriors after them. Singly and in groups they were dragged back to Falias the capital, in chains, until only one family remained free — the Windlords.

Tales of Paedur, the Bard

'Faolan...Faolan...Faolan...Wake up Faolan, they're here. Faolan...Faolan...Faolan, wake up. The Fomor are here!'

The boy jerked awake, the voice still echoing hollowly inside his head. He lay on the rough straw pallet, feeling his heart pounding in his chest — and then he realised that the pounding was coming from the corridor outside.

Faolan rolled off the bed and pulled on his boots. He pressed his face against the thick wooden door, but the sounds of doors opening and the metallic jingle of weapons and armour was too close. He ran to the slit window and peered through: he was six floors up, and even if there had been steps outside his window, he wouldn't have been able to slide though the narrow slit. He was trapped.

Sliding his knife from its sheath on his belt, the twelve-year-old boy prepared to meet his death.

A rumbling, grating sound made him turn, his huge golden eyes wide and frightened. As he watched, a long rectangular stone block slid out from the wall and shapes moved in the darkness beyond. Faolan's heart sank.

'Come on, come on. The Fomor are in the town.' It was Cian, his father. There was no fear in his voice, only anger.

'I know...I heard a voice...in my dream,' Faolan explained slowly.

'Tell me later. Now come on.' When Faolan squeezed past his

father, he found his mother and sister waiting in the narrow, draughty passage. Like him, they had slept in their clothes. This wasn't the first time they had fled in the night. Since they had fled Falias, the capital, a month ago, they had been pursued by the Emperor's Fomor warriors. So far they had been lucky to stay one step ahead of the serpent-folk. They had plans to head for one of the coastal towns, buy a boat and flee to the mysterious Eastern Isles, at the very edge of the known world. But with the Emperor's beasts hard on their heels, pressing them further and further inland, it didn't look as if they'd ever make it. They had arrived in Baddalaur, the ancient college town, two days previously, and had hoped to be able to rest up for a couple of days.

'Let's stay close together,' Cian, his father, advised. With the stone block back in place the passage was in total darkness. 'I'll lead the way.'

Etain, Faolan's mother and Grannia, his older sister followed, while Faolan took up the rear. The boy slid his knife out of its sheath; he knew it wouldn't do much against the tough hide or the leather armour of the Fomor, but it made him feel better.

'Where are we?' he asked, and although he had whispered, his voice sounded very loud in the confines of the tunnel.

'SShhhh,' Cian said softly. 'Although the Fomor's hearing is not very good, they can feel sounds.' He muttered a word and a spark appeared in the palm of his hand. Long shadows squirmed up the ancient-looking walls and across the curved ceiling. 'Baddalaur is one of the oldest of the De Danann towns,' he continued, consulting a tiny scrap of a map. 'It started as a single building — a school which specialised in training the famous warrior bards and scribes of legend. As the years passed, the town grew up around the school, and the school itself grew larger. Layer upon layer of buildings had been built around and sometimes on top of the older buildings. The result is that the entire college is riddled with hidden passages and lost corridors.'

'Does anything live down here?' Grannia asked nervously, glancing into the darkness.

'There are stories...' her father murmured. He nodded straight ahead. 'Hands on shoulders. Faolan, put your hand on your sister's shoulder. Etain, you hold mine. We go this way.' He closed his hand on the flame burning in his palm, extinguishing it, leaving them once again in absolute darkness. This was what it was like to be blind, Faolan realised. He took a deep breath, attempting to calm his thundering heart, and concentrated on his other senses. He was in a corridor, which was quite small in places because he could touch both sides. It was sloping downwards and the wind on his face was stale, carrying a hundred different unidentifiable odours. He had thought it would be completely silent in the corridor, but it seemed as if it was alive with sound. He could identify some of the noises: his family's footfalls echoing and re-echoing off the walls, the wind sighing and moaning up through the corridor, water dripping in the distance. But there were other less easily identifiable sounds: clickings, scratchings, distant moanings, a vague grumbling sound and once he heard a rasping slither as if something had crawled away close by.

He knew some of the legends that had grown up about these secret corridors, stories about students who had crept into the corridors to play some prank — and had never been seen or heard of again...except perhaps as a shape, a briefly-glimpsed terrifying semi-human shape. And what about the animals that were supposed to inhabit the very lowest levels of the corridors? Creatures of darkness, ghastly white because they never saw the sun, blind because they didn't need to see...

Faolan's fingers tightened on his sister's shoulder. He wondered how far they had to go.

*

A huge scaled fist smashed through the wooden door, splitting it from top to bottom. Another blow wrenched the door from its hinges, sending it flying across the room in two halves. The Fomor strode into the room, its flat serpent's head turning from side to side, forked tongue flickering, tasting the air. Its leather armour creaked as it moved slowly around the chill chamber. 'They've been here,' he hissed, 'four of the human-kind.' The creature's forked tongue darted out again, identifying the scents.

'Two of the adult kind, male and female. A young female, a young male.' The creature's yellow eyes looked around the chamber, which was bare except for an ancient bed, and then he pointed to the walls with his short-handled stabbing spear. 'Check the walls. There must be a hidden door.' The creature's laughter sounded like water steaming. 'Take this room apart, stone by stone if you have to. They haven't had time to escape,' he added triumphantly.

One of the Fomor warriors struck the wall with the haft of his spear. The stones rang solidly. He struck the wall again...and this time the sound was completely different.

'Here,' he hissed, striking the wall again. 'Behind this.'

Cichal, the leader of the Fomor warriors, an enormous battle-scarred creature who wore a metallic eye-patch over his left eye, strode forward and struck the wall with his fist. The stone boomed hollowly. Cichal hissed, the sound like water boiling, and struck the stone again. Dust and mortar drifted down from the ceiling.

'We have them now.' He reached for a war hammer. It resembled a carpenter's hammer, but it was built for a Fomor's claws and its stone head was as thick as a man's thigh. Holding the fearsome weapon in both hands, Cichal braced himself and then swung at the wall with all his might.

A huge section of the wall disintegrated under the massive blow, the sound vibrating through the entire building. The second blow ripped out the remainder of the wall. With a roar of triumph, Cichal stepped into the darkness.

*

The deep rumbling vibration stopped the humans in their tracks. A howl echoed down the tunnel, the sound absolutely terrifying as it rolled off the stones.

'Let's go.' Cian urged his wife and children forward with greater urgency. 'I didn't think they'd find the tunnels so easily.'

'Have we far to go?' Grannia whispered.

'Not far. I'd hoped to reach the underground river, but we're not going to make it. Our only chance now is to leave the tunnels and hope to lose the beasts in the college grounds. There's a doorway a little way ahead.'

'Windlordsssss....' The voice came down the tunnel in a long rasping hiss.

'Windlordsssss...there issss no essssscape....'

'Ignore them,' Cian muttered, 'say nothing. Their hearing is not good, they track mainly by smell.'

'I can hear youuuuuu, Windlordsssss. I can ssssmell your fear. I am coming for youuuu, Windlordsssss.' Faolan actually *felt* the hair on the back of his neck stand on end. He recognised Cichal's voice. He had often seen the Fomor standing behind the Emperor at state occasions. Even amongst his own people, Cichal was huge. A long scar ran down the left side of his face and the metallic eye-patch he wore made him even more terrifying-looking. The very fact that Cichal himself had been sent in pursuit of the Windlords was proof enough of how badly the Emperor wanted the secret of his parents' magic.

They raced on, moving deeper into the pitch-black tunnels. Faolan wondered how his parents could see: maybe their magic helped them see in the dark. And that gave him an idea.

'Magic!' he whispered urgently. 'Could you not use your magic to stop the beasts?'

'Don't be foolish,' Grannia snapped, 'even the most minor of spells takes care and preparation before it is worked.'

'Your sister is correct,' his mother said softly. 'But if the beasts get too close, they may find us harder to take than they imagined.'

'Hush now,' Cian muttered, and then he added, 'Shield your eyes.' Faolan squeezed his eyes shut. Through his closed lids, he saw a tall orange rectangle. Without thinking he opened his eyes and then moaned as a brilliant light blinded him; fire was sparking from his father's fingers, biting deep into the stone, cutting out the shape of a door. Standing back, his father lashed out with his foot, and a whole section of the wall fell away. Light streamed into the tunnel. Blinking tears from his eyes, Faolan was helped out of the tunnel by his sister and mother, while his father gathered up the fallen stones and piled them into the opening. Kneeling on the floor, he ran his hands over the stones. They turned semi-liquid and flowed like thick mud, filling up the cracks.

'It won't fool anyone from this side,' the tall, grey-haired man murmured, looking at the mess, 'but it may fool the Fomor from the other side.' He turned and smiled at his family. 'And then again, it may not. The Fomor are not stupid. Never judge a creature by its looks,' he added.

They had come out of the tunnel into the main hall of Baddalaur's principal library, one of the oldest buildings in the city. The building was circular and rose up eight floors to a beautifully painted ceiling. The shelves ran around the walls, and the higher one went, the older the books and maps, scrolls, charts, tablets and papyri became. Only the most senior librarians and respected scholars were allowed access to the top two floors. The ground floor was also shelved, and long broad tables ran the length of the room. There were numerous books scattered along the tables. Faolan ran his hands across his blurring eyes and looked around in wonder. The Library at Baddalaur was one of the wonders of the modern world; legend had it that if a man were to read all the books in the library he would become a god.

His father grabbed him by the arm and pointed to the stairs which Etain and Grannia had already reached, their bright gold hair brilliant in the dusty light.

'Come on Faolan, this is no time for day-dreaming. We'll come back and look around another time.' Faolan and his father had reached the stairs when the Fomor smashed through the door and burst out of the narrow tunnel, showering dust and stones into the circular room.

Cichal howled in triumph. 'I have you now, Windlord.' The serpent lifted its short spear and hurled it at the man and boy even though they were on the other side of the room.

Cian grabbed his son by the collar and hauled him upwards — just as the spear splintered through the stairs at his feet.

From the balcony, Faolan saw six of the serpent-folk sprint

across the floor, their spiked tails slithering and rasping along the smoothly polished flagstones. Although he couldn't read their inhuman expressions, he thought they looked as if they were smiling.

'I have you now,' Cichal roared as he neared the stairs. He dragged his sword free of its shoulder harness. The weapon was as tall as a man, with a broad, leaf-shaped blade that had been honed from a slab of grey stone.

'Not yet, Fomor,' Cian shouted. 'You forget; I am the Wind-lord.' Taking a deep breath, he closed his eyes and raised his hands high. Faolan threw himself to the floor and covered his head with his hands. He knew what his father was going to do...

Alison turned her back on her brother and looked out across the
flat, metallic-looking Atlantic Ocean. Squinting against the late
afternoon sunshine, she took a deep breath, tasting the salt and
seaweed on the air. Where she was standing on the top of the
island, over five hundred feet above the waves, the air was so
cold it burned her lungs and the wind made her eyes water. It
was a strange feeling to realise that she was standing on the
westernmost part of Ireland — next stop America, she thought.
Alison turned back to her brother. 'We should go down, Ken,
there's a fog rising off the sea.'

Kenneth sat with his back to the high stone wall, carefully
cutting a series of long jagged rents in his new jeans with his
pocket-knife. 'What time is it?' he asked, testing the edge of his
knife against his thumb. The tough denim had blunted the blade.

Ally pushed strands of her copper-red hair off her forehead
and tilted back her sun-glasses with a smoothly practised move.
She was fourteen, a year and a month older than her brother, and
liked to think herself much more sophisticated. It annoyed her
immensely when people mistook them for twins, although with
their red hair and pale green eyes and because they were a similar
height, it was an easy mistake to make. She glanced at her Swatch
watch. 'It's five,' she muttered. 'We've at least another half an
hour on this god-forsaken island,' she sighed.

Ken folded away his knife and stood up to admire the effect

of the slashes he had cut in his jeans. White flesh showed through the holes. 'Not bad eh? What do you think?'

'Let's see what Mum and Dad think,' Ally sneered. 'Those jeans are less than a week old — and you only got them because your old jeans were in shreds.'

'I liked those old jeans; it took me ages to get them that way. In any case, Mum and Dad never notice what I'm wearing. I could be in fancy dress and they wouldn't bat an eyelid.' Ken straightened and stretched his arms wide, breathing in the ice-cold salty air. 'We'd better head back down. I didn't realise we'd climbed so high.'

'Six hundred and seventy steps,' Ally said bitterly. 'And for what? A bunch of old ruins. We shouldn't have stayed.'

'I thought it was interesting,' Ken remarked looking around. They were standing in the midst of the ancient monastic settlement on top of the isle of Skellig Michael, off the south-west coast of Kerry.

'Yeah, interesting for an hour maybe,' Ally snapped. 'But when you've seen one stone hut, you've seen them all.'

'Well there were the gannets, and the puffins...'

'They weren't puffins,' Ally interrupted.

'They looked like puffins to me. Anyway, it was more exciting than being stuck on that boat. Anything is more exciting than that. No,' he shook his head, 'I thought it was interesting.'

'That's why you've spent the last hour slicing up your jeans,' Ally said triumphantly, determined to have the last word. They had never been the best of friends, even as young children, and now that they were attending separate boarding schools, where they had their own friends and interests, they had become almost strangers to one another. Neither had wanted to come on this holiday in the first place, and they showed their resentment by constantly bickering and arguing, which had driven their parents mad.

Ken shrugged, admitting defeat. 'Okay, okay. We saw it all in an hour. And we have been here a long time...'

'We've been here all day,' Ally reminded him. 'And even if the boat gets back here on time, it's a two-hour sail to Knightstown. Some holiday this has turned out to be,' she grumbled.

'Look, don't bite my head off. I can't do anything about it, can I? If you've got a complaint, talk to Mum and Dad.'

Ally walked away from her brother and leaned against the crude stone wall, looking down at the grey blanket of fog that now obscured the waves, far below. 'Ken, we've stopped at every castle, every lake, every standing stone and high cross, and every mound of dirt on the road from Dublin.'

Ken sighed. 'I know, I know. But they're historians, what do you expect? It's all part of the research for their book,' he said, defending them.

'This isn't a holiday,' Ally said bitterly. 'A holiday is sun and sand, lying by the pool with a cold drink. A holiday is having parents you see every day for a couple of hours.' She marched off, moving through the small stone huts that had once housed the monks who had lived and prayed on Skellig Michael. 'Well, I've had enough,' she called back over her shoulder, 'I'm sick and tired of this.'

Kenneth shook his head and puffed out his cheeks in a sigh. He couldn't disagree with what his sister was saying, but at least he had some interest in the history and mythology of his native land: his sister had none.

Their parents, Gillian and Robert Morand, were researching a new book, *The Monastic Tradition in Ireland*, during the school holidays. They were both University lecturers and had little opportunity during term-time to put their theories to the test, to make measurements and take photographs.

Gillian Morand had attempted to interest them in the book as they drove across Ireland. She explained that they were hoping to prove that most, if not all, of the Christian remains, the burial grounds, the high crosses, the monasteries and churches, were in fact built upon the ruins of older pagan sites. It wasn't a new theory, Robert had added, but they believed that some form of pagan worship had been carried on in these places even after they had been claimed by the Christian Church.

They were especially interested in the remote monastic settlements, most of which were only accessible by sea. They had hired a yacht in Cobh and then worked their way from Kinsale to the Blaskets and Valentia Island. The Skelligs were their final destination.

They had left Knightstown on the first tide earlier that morning. They had actually reached Skellig Michael when the wind had died away and their inboard engine refused to start. Given the choice of returning under sail to Valentia for repairs or remaining for a picnic on the island close by, Ken and Ally, only too delighted to be off the heaving boat, had chosen to row into the natural slipway in the rubber dinghy with their father. The Atlantic swell meant that they had to jump from the dinghy onto the slipway or risk tearing the rubber on the barnacle-encrusted landing point.

'We'll try to be back by half past five at the latest,' Robert had shouted as he rowed strongly away, straining against the pull of the current. By the time Ken and Ally had reached the top steps, the yacht was underway and the island was theirs for the rest of the day.

They had picnicked at the automatic lighthouse before making the long climb up to the ancient stone huts. On a gentle slope they had come across a large headstone which marked the grave of the wife and three children of the lighthouse keeper, all of whom had died in the same year, a hundred years and more ago. Ally and Ken had looked at one another and moved on, both of them chilled by the simple stone, and continued on upwards to the monks' settlement in silence, wondering about the simple marker.

Ken took a last look around the little terrace with its collection of five beehive-shaped stone huts, each one standing on a different level, and decided that his parents' theory didn't work here. There were six of these huts on the island, as well as two tiny oratories where the monks would have gathered in prayer. There were several stone crosses dotted around the island, and two wells. He doubted that this had ever been anything other than a Christian monastery.

'Are you coming or not?' Ally reappeared from behind one of the huts.

'I'm coming. I'm coming. You could have gone on,' he added, and then teased, '...or were you afraid to go down on your own?'

'Don't be stupid,' she snapped. 'The steps are damp and I didn't want to risk falling,' she finished lamely.

Ken joined his sister at the top of the stone steps and looked down. Although they were standing in bright sunshine, the lower portion of the island was wrapped in cloud. They were five hundred and forty feet above the landing site, and he could just about make out the lighthouse buildings close to the jetty.

'It'll be cold in the clouds,' he remarked, pulling his jumper from around his waist and slipping it on.

'We're going to freeze on that stupid boat going back.' Ally shivered in anticipation of the long sail back to the mainland. 'I hope Mum and Dad are OK in the fog,' she added as she pulled her cardigan off her shoulders, slid her arms into the sleeves and buttoned it up.

'It shouldn't take us too long to get down,' Ken said as they set off down the well-worn smooth steps.

'Well, they're hardly likely to go without us, are they?' Ally remarked sarcastically. 'Although,' she added, 'they just might. Sometimes I think they forget all about us.'

Ken said nothing; he had often thought the same himself.

'In fact, I sometimes think they'd be far happier living a thousand years in the past.'

Ken shook his head. 'Make that two thousand,' he said with a grin. 'One...' he began, stepping onto the first step.

'Two...' Ally continued.

'Three...'

*

At its highest point Skellig Michael rises seven hundred and fifteen feet above sea level. The monastic ruins stand at about five hundred and forty feet above sea level and are reached by six hundred and seventy stone steps.

The clouds closed in when they reached step one hundred.

By step one-sixty, they were completely enclosed in a thick, bitterly cold damp mist.

By step two hundred, they could scarcely see three or four steps ahead of them.

Although the thick clouds around them had swallowed the other sounds they had grown used to throughout the day — the cries of the countless sea birds, the ever-present rush and roar of the sea, the distant booming of the waves against the cliffs — they could still hear the wind howling around the island.

And, although the wind seemed to be rising, they couldn't actually feel it on their skins or hair. The air smelt different too: gone were the sharp and clean salt and iodine odours of the sea, now they could smell something sweeter, like herbs or spices, or rotting fruit.

When they reached step seven hundred, they looked at one another, imagining they'd made a mistake and miscounted.

By the time they reached the eight-hundredth step, they knew something was very wrong.

Cian raised his arms and called the wind with a word.

For a single moment nothing happened, and then abruptly, it was as if all the air had been sucked from the room, leaving a complete and terrifying silence. It lasted for the space of a single heartbeat, but when the air returned, it came in a deafening bang that shook the entire building. A howling wind swept across the floor of the library. It ripped the books from the shelves and sent them hurtling against the Fomor.

'I am the Windlord,' Cian said simply and the wind took and magnified his voice, sending it booming around the room. The storm grew in intensity as he spoke and was now visible as a greyish mist in the centre of the floor. 'I am the Lord of the Air; Master of the Wind.'

Whole sections of shelving were ripped free, their contents streaming through the air. Books, some of them covered in cloth and leather, or wood and hide, some bound in metal or thin slivers of stone, others wrapped in human skin, spun around the room in the tightly whirling tornado.

Cichal howled as the blizzard struck him, his great sword instinctively lashing out, slicing an enormous atlas in two. A series of large law books, each one bound in wood, struck him across the chest and head, sending him staggering backwards. He smashed into a bookcase in the middle of the floor, sending it toppling to the ground. The beast lost his footing and crashed down on top of it.

The air was filled with books now, spinning, twisting, turning, coiling, forcing the Fomor backwards towards the opening of the tunnel. The numerous volumes began to pile up around the entrance, blocking the hole. One of the serpent-folk broke through the barrier and ran screaming towards the steps leading up to the Windlords, but a metal-bound prayer-book struck him across the shins, doubling him over, and then a reading table crashed into him, actually picking him up off the ground, sending him tumbling across the polished floor.

Cichal crouched on all fours, using his barbed tail to help him keep his balance, digging his talons into the stone floor. The wind was a physical thing, stronger than the strongest warrior, pushing him backwards, his razor-sharp claws leaving deep furrows in the stone. The books were like slingshots, sharp, stinging and deadly. His six warriors were a match for a hundred of the human-kind, but they had no way of fighting the invisible elemental magic. When the Emperor had told him to bring back this wind magician, Cichal had been almost insulted. There were other magicians, magicians who could raise the dead, command fire and stone, control demons — these were magicians with power, not some Windlord, whose only magic was to make the wind blow.

But crouched on the floor of Baddalaur's ancient library, bruised and bleeding, while the four human-kind fled higher into the building, Cichal understood the power of this wind magic.

Whoever controlled this power, controlled the world.

The Fomor smashed his fist into the floor, shattering a stone slab: there was nothing he could do...except wait. No magician could keep a spell working indefinitely.

*

'Help me,' Faolan gasped, staggering up the stairs, hauling the limp body of his father. The young boy's eyes were bright with tears. 'One moment he was fine, and then he just collapsed.'

Grannia came around her father's left side and draped his arm over her shoulder, while Etain raised her husband's head and lifted an eyelid. Only the white was showing.

'Lay your father here.' She swept a book-laden table free with her arm and together the three of them managed to lift Cian up onto the table. Etain lifted his wrist and felt for his pulse. It was faint and ragged. 'What happened, Faolan?' she asked. 'Tell me exactly what happened.'

'He had called up the wind and used it to drive the Fomor back,' Faolan began.

'How did he call up the wind?' Etain interrupted.

The boy looked at her in surprise. 'He just raised his hands and began.'

Etain drew in a sharp breath, tears magnifying her eyes.

'Mother...mother? What's wrong?' Faolan demanded, but it was Grannia who answered. She had already begun her training in the Windlore, and knew some of the dangers involved in raising the wind.

'You cannot call the wind just like that,' she said quietly. 'It needs time and preparation. The Windlore is one of the four elemental magics, like fire, earth and water. It draws its power from within the magician, unlike other forms of magic which use special ingredients. If the magician isn't prepared physically and mentally to work the spell, then the elemental magic will destroy him. It will just use him up.' Her eyes darted to the unconscious form of her father. His chest was barely moving and there was blood on his lips. She looked at her mother. 'What are we going to do?'

Etain shook her head. 'I don't know,' she said tiredly.

There was a sudden crash from below and Faolan ran to the railing, looking down into the devastated hallway below. The Fomor had broken out of the tunnel again and were now advancing through the rubble towards the steps.

'They're coming,' he gasped. 'We've got to go...'

'Your father cannot be moved,' Etain said firmly.

'But the Fomor...' Grannia began.

'The Fomor want us alive; they won't harm us. They know if anything happens to us, the Emperor will have their heads.'

'But what are we going to do?' Faolan whispered. They could hear the beasts' claws rasping on the wooden stairs.

'You two will have to flee...' Both Grannia and Faolan started to shake their heads, but Etain pressed on. 'Go north into the Ice-Fields of Thusal. In a village close to the Top of the World you'll find your uncle, Lugh. He is the last of the Windriders. Give him this.' She pressed a small ancient-looking book into Faolan's hands. 'This is the Book of the Wind. It is so ancient that legend has it that the gods themselves wrote it. It contains the Windlore; whoever reads this book will know the secret of the wind. They could become a Windlord. It must not fall into the Emperor's hands. Find your uncle, tell him what has happened; tell him we need his help now.' She leaned over and kissed them both, 'Now go. Go!'

Both Grannia and Faolan shook their heads.

'You have to go,' Etain insisted. 'The wind is the most powerful of the elemental magics; if the Emperor controls it, he can control the world.'

'I'm staying,' Grannia said simply. She looked at Faolan. 'You go. One person will have a better chance of evading the beasts than two, and besides, you know no magic. They won't be able to track you that way.'

Puzzled, Faolan looked at his mother.

'Every little use of magic disturbs the natural world, like a pebble dropped into a pool,' Etain explained. 'A good magician will be able to track another user of magic across many hundreds of leagues. Grannia is right. She has used magic, she would be easy to track.' Etain reached out her hand and held it close to her daughter's face. 'I can feel the power flowing off her from here.' She leaned forward and kissed her son on the forehead. 'You'll have to go alone, Faolan. You are our only hope.'

The beasts were so close now that they could smell their sour, snake smell.

'Go now, Faolan. Protect the book with your life. Whatever you do, don't let it fall into the Emperor's hands...destroy it if you have to, but only as a last resort. Now go! We'll try to hold them here.'

Blinking furiously, Faolan came to his feet. The Fomor were on the stairs, moving cautiously now that they had learned of the Windlord's power. He kissed his mother quickly and hugged his sister, and then he leaned across his father and kissed his cold, clammy cheek. 'I'll be back,' he whispered into his ear. 'I'll come back for you.'

He barely made it to the stairs before the Fomor burst onto the landing.

*

The Fomor Officer stopped at the top of the stairs, his huge sword held in both claws, and looked at the humans. It was a trap. After the devastating attack on the ground floor, he had led his troop up the stairs with extreme caution. A man who could control that much power might be able to rip the staircase away from the wall and send them tumbling to the ground. Out of his original troop of six, only four were mobile. One was unconscious and another had broken a leg when a shelf full of heavy books had fallen on him.

Cichal had been expecting an attack: he hadn't been expecting to find one of the human-kind lying injured and bleeding on a table, with the two females standing close by, offering no resistance.

His forked tongue flicked out, sorting through the scents, the odours now confused by the bitter stench of blood, both from the human-kind and his own troops, and the peculiar bitter-sweet, herbal odour of magic that hung in the air.

There was one missing.

When they had tracked the human-kind to the tower room he had identified four human odours, two adult, two young. One of the young was missing. The creature was probably unimportant, but nevertheless...

'One of the whelps has escaped us,' he spoke to his lieutenant in the sharp hissing tongue of the Fomor. 'He cannot have gone far. Bring him back.'

'Unharmed?' the huge scarred warrior asked with a leer.

'Alive, Meng,' Cichal snapped. 'I don't care what condition he's in. These are the important ones.' He turned to look at the two women, and switched to the human tongue. 'You were foolish to run,' he hissed, in the peculiar lisping accent of the Fomor. 'The Emperor requests the pleasure of your company.'

'My husband is ill,' Etain said quickly, interrupting him. 'Find him a doctor.'

Cichal stepped up to the woman. He towered above her and he had to bend his head to look down at her. His mouth opened, revealing three rows of triangular teeth, designed for tearing raw meat. His bad breath made Etain gag. 'You are not in a position to demand anything, human.'

'Your Emperor wants us alive,' she said firmly. 'Especially my husband,' she gasped, breathing through her mouth in an attempt to avoid the creature's foul smell. 'Now there are many doctors here in Baddalaur. I'd suggest you find one...and quickly.'

Cichal glared at the woman and then he stepped back and snapped a quick command. 'Find a doctor.' Planting his sword point first in the wooden floor, resting both hands on the cross-hilt, he allowed himself to relax. He had achieved what two other troops of Fomor, and two garrisons of the Emperor's human troops had failed to do: he had captured the Windlords. He looked at the two women standing protectively over the unconscious body of the man, and then he glanced upwards at the next floor. What was keeping Meng?

*

Meng was thinking about meat...human meat. He hadn't eaten human meat in a long time. It was illegal of course, but there were inns in the back streets of Falias, the capital, which served human flesh to connoisseurs like himself.

He wondered what a young boy would taste like.

His fleshy tongue darted out, tasting the air, following the scents of sweat and fear from the boy, the odours of the leather and wool that he wore. Meng moved down the long corridor. To

25

his left he could see out over the balustrade down into the main library hall, three floors below. To his right there was nothing but shelf after shelf of books. Further down the corridor, there was a stairway leading up to the next floor: no doubt the boy had gone that way.

Meng looked at the books again, rubbing a long hooked talon down the spines as he walked past, ripping through the leather and paper. The human-kind were a weak, puny race. Soft of flesh and bone, easily broken. They put down their words on stone and wood, leather, leaves and now paper, recording their history, their geography, their myths and legends. To read their literature was to learn of their weakness, their mistakes...to learn how they might be taken. There was no written tradition amongst the Fomor; each Fomor whelp learned the lore and legends of their race by heart. So long as one of the Fomor remained alive, then the Fomor culture could be recreated. Meng pulled out a book and shredded a five-hundred-year-old collection of legends: if this library were to be destroyed, then much of the human-kind's knowledge would go with it. They called themselves the People of the Goddess, but if the gods of the human-kind really existed, then they too must be weak and puny if they accepted the worship of such a race.

He stopped at the foot of the stairs, listening, turning his head from side to side to catch any sounds. The Fomors' hearing was poor, as was their sight, but it was more than compensated for by their excellent sense of smell. He tasted the air, and then hissed in satisfaction. The boy was above. As he mounted the stairs, he slid free a dagger with long ragged teeth set into one side of the blade. Maybe he'd cut himself a slice of the boy...just for a little taste...

*

Faolan leaned all his weight against the bookshelf. For a moment it resisted and then abruptly ripped free from the wall and crashed down across the staircase, sending hundreds of volumes cascading down the stairs onto the Fomor. The boy laughed aloud as he heard the creature tumble down the steps, and then he turned and ran.

He tried to work out how he was going to get out of the library. The Great College formed the heart of Baddalaur. It had originally been built on a hill, and the town had grown up around it, as merchants and shopkeepers had moved in to provide goods and services for the growing community of teachers, scholars and students who crowded into the building. As the years passed, the college continued to grow and needed even more space, but since the fields surrounding it were already covered with shops and houses, it could only grow upwards. At eight floors high, the Library was the tallest building in the town. Faolan counted quickly. He was more than half way to the top; he didn't even want to think about what would happen when he reached the top floor where the observatory was.

He needed some place to hide...or a weapon...or some way to distract the creature...or some way to mask his own smell.

Hiding was out of the question. He knew he could dodge in and around these bookstacks, but sooner or later the Fomor, who could track him by smell, would catch up with him. A weapon would be useless against the creature. He thought briefly about fire, but shook his head. Fire would devastate the building and destroy its priceless collection of books and maps.

There was nothing for him to do but continue climbing.

Faolan turned at the stairs leading up to the sixth floor and looked back. He was in time to see the Fomor's flat serpent's head peer over the edge of the stairs. It hissed when it spotted him, and lifted a wicked-looking knife.

'Come to me, little boy. Don't make me chase you.'

Faolan reached for the nearest book — an ancient wooden map case, with brass hinges — and flung it at the creature. The sharp edge struck it on the bony ridge just above the eye, leaving a small cut. Pale pink fluid seeped from the wound.

'That was a mistake, boy,' Meng hissed. Its tail lashed angrily from side to side as it advanced down the corridor. 'I was supposed to bring you back alive. But I think you're about to have a fatal accident.' Long tendrils of saliva dribbled from the corner of the creature's mouth, and Faolan had a very good idea of what was going to happen to him. Everyone knew that the Fomor stole human children and ate them.

Faolan turned and ran, racing down the long corridor on the sixth level. He tossed over free-standing bookshelves, overturned reading stands and tables, creating a tangled mess for the large-footed creature to wade through.

Faolan had actually reached the steps leading up to the seventh level when the Fomor caught up with him.

The creature had been gaining steadily and Faolan had been tiring. He could smell the creature's stink as it closed on him, and he could feel his shoulders tense where he expected the blow to fall.

He threw himself at the stairs, jumping straight onto the third step — just as the creature lunged with its dagger. The blade sliced through the heel of Faolan's boot, ripping it away. The boy lashed out at the Fomor with his foot, catching it under the jaw. Its teeth clicked solidly together, giving Faolan precious moments to climb higher. He was just beginning to think he'd make it to the next level, when the Fomor's claws closed around his ankle and he was dragged down the wooden stairs.

Meng pressed the tip of his knife to Faolan's throat. 'That long chase has made me very hungry...'

'We didn't count them right,' Ally said softly, unable to keep her voice steady.

'Maybe,' Ken agreed, though privately he didn't think so.

'How many steps is it now?'

'Nine hundred and two,' he said quietly.

'That's impossible,' Ally breathed.

'I know it is.'

'What are we going to do?' She lifted her arm and squinted through the grey swirling mist at the watch on her wrist. She rubbed the sleeve of her cardigan across the face, wiping off the water droplets. Her digital watch showed 5:18. She stared at it, puzzled; when she'd looked at it at least five minutes ago, she thought it had said 5:17. Maybe the moisture in the air was affecting it, although the watch was supposed to be waterproof. 'Ken, what are we going to do?' she repeated.

He shook his head. 'I don't know.' He ran both hands through his copper-red hair, pushing it back off his face. The spikes it had taken him an hour to arrange now hung limp and twisted with the moisture, and the setting gel he'd used was dripping down his face in sticky streamers. He rubbed his tacky hands on his jumper. He was cold, starting to shiver, and he regretted slicing up his jeans. 'I suppose we could go back up ...'

'We've already come down nine hundred steps.' Ally's voice sounded hoarse. She coughed and cleared her throat. 'How many steps are there supposed to be?'

'Six hundred and seventy,' he said softly. He turned and looked back, but the thick enveloping mist only allowed him to see two steps in any direction. 'I'm not sure if I could climb back up in any case. My legs feel rubbery.'

Ally nodded. Her calf and thigh muscles were aching. 'So we go down.'

Ken shrugged. 'Looks like it.'

'But how far do we go?' she wondered.

'All the way,' he said seriously.

Ally bit the inside of her cheeks, determined not to let the tears show. 'Do you know any stories about Skellig Michael?' she asked nervously.

'All of them,' Ken grinned.

'Any scary ones: is the island haunted?'

'The ghosts of the long-dead monks are supposed to walk the steps at night, climbing endlessly from top to bottom.'

'You're joking,' she said, watching him closely.

'Of course I am.'

Ally didn't believe him.

'Nine hundred and ninety-eight...nine hundred and ninety-nine...one thousand!' Ken slumped down on the step and wrapped his arms around his thin body. He was shivering from a combination of fright and exhaustion. Ally sat down beside him and draped an arm across his shoulders. He rested his head back against her arm.

'This is like some sort of bad dream.' His voice was barely above a whisper. 'I keep thinking these steps will end. I keep hoping that with the next step the clouds will open up and we'll find ourselves at the bottom.'

Ally nodded: she'd been thinking, hoping, praying for the same thing.

'Maybe we should rest for a while and then turn back,' he suggested.

'I couldn't face climbing a thousand steps,' Ally said firmly. 'No, we'll continue down. It has to lead somewhere.'

'Straight to hell probably,' Ken muttered.

Meng the Fomor wrapped his claws in the front of Faolan's jerkin and lifted him straight off the ground. The knife never left his throat. 'Don't struggle boy, you'll cut yourself,' the creature hissed.

The Fomor moved swiftly upwards, its broad feet slipping on the narrow wooden stairs that had been built for the feet of men. He needed to put as much distance as possible between himself and the rest of the Troop, otherwise the scent of blood would bring them. He paced along the corridor of the seventh level with the boy tucked under one arm, looking for a room or a chamber beside an open window where fresh air would help disperse the salt odour of fresh blood. He knew he didn't have much time; Cichal would be sure to send someone up after him...but Meng was determined that he wasn't sharing this tasty morsel with anyone.

There were no rooms on the seventh floor, so he climbed up to the eighth and top floor. The creature hissed its peculiar laugh. This was the highest point in the library. It was situated in the tip of the tower and was therefore smaller than any of the other floors. He looked at the strange instruments in the room before he realised that it was now used as an observatory. Hinged metal plates covered the tall arched windows, and the entire roof was composed of a series of interleaved wooden slats. Long barrelled tubes and peculiar metal instruments were strewn about on the narrow table that almost completely encircled the room. There were glasses and lenses everywhere and an enormous metal cylinder dominated the centre of the floor. It was on wheels and set into a series of tracks on the floor.

This place was perfect.

Ramming his knife back into its sheath high on his chest, Meng hurried around the room, sliding open each of the twelve windows, allowing the early morning light to burn into the room. The view out over Baddalaur and the surrounding countryside was spectacular, but neither Meng nor Faolan appreciated it. With the knife gone from his throat, Faolan was concentrating on trying to reach his small belt pouch. This Fomor might be going to kill and eat him, but he wasn't going to give up without a fight.

The Fomor stared at the roof, wondering how to open it. It took a few moments before he realised that the circular wheel by the door was connected to a series of wires that were connected to the roof. Adjusting his grip on the boy, the Fomor gripped the wheel in his talons and spun it savagely. The wooden slats rattled half-way across the roof and then jammed. Meng spun the wheel in the opposite direction, but the overlapping slats were stuck fast.

No matter. There was enough cold air in the room to blow away the rich meaty odour of blood. Sweeping a section of the table free with his arm he dropped the boy onto it and pulled out his knife. He was wondering why the whelp didn't seem frightened when he realised that the human-kind was looking past him...

The dark-haired, dark-eyed boy had appeared behind the Fomor without a sound. His leather jerkin and trousers were a deep dark brown and he wore the triangular eye and pyramid design of a bard high on his left shoulder. There was a circle around the badge which indicated that he was an apprentice. He looked at Faolan for a second and then raised a long thin finger to his lips before stepping back to the huge telescope in the middle of the floor. He worked swiftly at the wheels and cogs and Faolan was just beginning to wonder what the mysterious boy was going to do when the Fomor realised he wasn't paying attention and looked around...

The telescope hit Meng across the side of the head with a solid thump that left a huge indentation in its metallic body. The beast was thrown across the room, crashing onto a table, scattering glass and metal instruments across the floor.

The apprentice bard grabbed Faolan and hauled him off the table just as the Fomor staggered to his feet. The beast was covered in a score of tiny nicks and cuts and the right side of his face looked slightly out of shape. He spat on the floor, and a dozen triangular teeth spilled onto the ground. Reaching behind his shoulder he hauled his broad-bladed stone sword free.

'Have you got a plan?' Faolan gasped.

'Hitting the creature on the head was my plan. He was not supposed to get up,' the young bard said quietly, his voice surprisingly rich and musical. Faolan frowned; the voice sounded almost familiar.

The Fomor backed the two boys towards the tall open windows, his sword moving to and fro in front of his body, keeping them at bay. He suddenly lunged forward and lashed out with his sword.

It happened so fast that Faolan didn't even see the blade coming. There was an explosion of sparks before his face. The broad blade of the Fomor's sword had been stopped a finger length away from his face by a narrow-bladed hook the bard held in his left hand...and then Faolan suddenly realised that the other boy wasn't holding it. He had no left hand: the hook took the place of his hand.

The young bard twisted his hook and the sword fell away. The Fomor stepped back and took a two-handed grip on the enormous sword. 'Try that trick again boy, and I'll rip your arm off.' He looked at the two human-kind; the golden-haired, golden-eyed one and the dark-haired, dark-eyed, one-handed one...and he wondered if they would taste different. He saw the golden-haired whelp pull open his belt pouch and pluck out a small round stone. His lips drew back from his teeth in a smile: what was the whelp going to do, throw it at him?

The small blue egg-like stone shattered against the Fomor's leather breastplate and a pale green sticky gum dripped down the front of the armour. A smell like rotten eggs filled the room, and then the gum popped alight!

Meng had his sword above his head when the flames appeared before his eyes, scorching the sensitive flesh beneath his jaw. Foul-smelling smoke coiled into his nostrils and open mouth. He staggered backwards and dropped the sword, patting the flames with his claws. But the sticky gum clung to his claws and burnt into the hard flesh.

The Fomor were terrified of fire; it was one of the few things they had no defence against; burnt scales and flesh would never grow again.

Throwing back his head the creature howled, a long, terrified, hissing scream that echoed and re-echoed off the walls.

The bard grabbed Faolan by the arm and dragged him towards one of the open windows. 'We must go. Every Fomor in Baddalaur will have heard that cry.' He glanced back over his shoulder at the Fomor who was still beating at the flames on his breastplate with his burning hands. 'The firestone sap will soon burn itself out, and I do not think either of us should be around when that happens.' The bard leaned out over the window and pointed downwards. 'I hope you have a head for heights.'

Faolan leaned over the window-ledge and looked down. A series of narrow stone steps had been added onto the side of the tower. They led straight down, over the town walls and disappeared into the thick swirling mists that covered the Baddalaur Marshlands which lay on the north side of the town.

'There's no railing, nothing to hold onto,' Faolan murmured, feeling his fingers and toes beginning to tingle.

'You can always stay here,' the bard said, his thin lips twisting in a smile.

They could both near the noisy clatter of the Fomor as they pounded up the stairs.

Faolan glanced over the edge again. 'Is it a long way down?'

'Fifteen hundred steps.'

Faolan swallowed hard, and then he stretched out his right

hand. 'My name is Faolan.'

The bard stretched out his right hand and grasped Faolan's arm at the elbow. 'I know who you are, Windlord. It was I who warned you this morning that the Fomor were coming.' He grinned at Faolan's startled expression.

Faolan suddenly remembered the voice that had invaded his dream, *'Faolan...Faolan...Faolan...Wake up Faolan, they're here. Faolan...Faolan...Faolan, wake up. The Fomor are here!'* No wonder the bard's voice had sounded familiar.

'I am Paedur, apprentice bard. There'll be time for questions later.' He jumped up onto the window-ledge, hauling Faolan up after him. Stepping out onto the first narrow step, he pressed his back against the wall, the hook that took the place of his left hand ringing off the stone. He reached up for Faolan's hand.

'Look at me. Keep your eyes on me. Look neither up nor down.'

Faolan immediately looked down over the edge...and felt his stomach surge up into his mouth. Beads of sweat popped out on his forehead and his hands were immediately damp with sweat. He was standing on a step that had obviously been built for the Small Folk, the Cluricaun or Fir Dearg from the forests of the south. It was so narrow he couldn't put both feet on the same step and even with his heel pressed back against the step, more than half of his foot was sticking out over the air. Below him there was nothing but a grey-white mass that looked soft enough to fall into. Only the tops of the tallest trees poking through the surface of the cloud destroyed the illusion.

'Is this safe,' he whispered hoarsely, his mouth dry.

'A lot safer than staying in the room,' Paedur smiled.

*

Cichal stormed into the observatory, the enormous stone sword in his hand. He stopped when he saw Meng crouched on the floor amidst the devastation of broken bottles and twisted metal, cradling blackened and burnt claws. The Fomor's breastplate was also scorched and charred.

'What happened?' Cichal hissed.

Meng rocked to and fro, aware only of the pain in his burnt claws.

'Report, Fomor!' Cichal snapped.

'He escaped, Officer,' Meng replied, the words hissed through clenched teeth. 'A one-handed youth aided him. They burnt me with a firestone,' he added.

Cichal grabbed Meng by the throat and hauled him to his feet. 'You allowed two of the human-kind — both of them whelps — to defeat you? You are not worthy to belong to the Emperor's troop. Where did you last see them?' he demanded.

'They were standing by the window, Officer.'

Cichal dropped the Fomor and strode to the window. Leaning out, he immediately spotted the two human boys about twenty steps below. They were both pressed flat against the wall, staring anxiously upward. Without turning around, he snapped, 'I want two Fomor waiting for them at the bottom of the steps. See to it.' He looked over his shoulder and pointed to the archer. 'You! Kill the dark-haired one. Perhaps we can frighten the other whelp into coming back up to us of his own accord.'

The Fomor archer fitted a short, broad-headed arrow to his immensely powerful bow and leaned out over the window-ledge. 'It is a difficult shot, Officer,' he hissed, his flicking tongue testing the direction of the wind. The angle of the curving wall made the shot particularly awkward.

'Do it!' Cichal snapped.

The archer drew the bowstring back to his scaled jaw and fired. The air whistled through tiny slits cut into the head of the arrow, making a screaming whistle as it sped towards Faolan and Paedur.

'It was a seagull,' Ally said shakily.

'That was no seagull,' Ken said firmly.

'I know,' Ally admitted.

The object had appeared from above. It had come screaming down through the mists and disappeared off to their right. It was the first sound they had heard since they had entered the chill cloud...and it had terrified them both.

'I wonder what it was,' Ken began, and then stopped abruptly. The noise had begun again.

It was a high-pitched whistling scream, the screech a blade of grass makes when it is pressed between thumbs and then blown through.

Something howled out of the mist above their heads and shattered onto one of the stone steps behind them. Two pieces of broken wood rolled down the steps to land at their feet.

Ken stooped and picked them up. He fitted them together without a word and showed the result to his sister.

'It's an arrow,' she whispered. She looked up into the grey mist. 'Do you mean there's someone up there firing arrows down at us? That's ridiculous.' She looked at the long arrow again. It might be ridiculous, but it was happening. 'But what's making the screaming sound?' she muttered, almost to herself.

Ken turned the broad pyramidal-shaped arrow head and blew gently at it. It whistled softly. 'The screaming was made as the air blew through these slits.'

'Who fired these, Ken?'

'And why?' he asked, although his heart was pounding so hard he had difficulty talking. 'I'm not staying here to find out. Come on.'

Ally hesitated, unsure what to do, until another arrow screamed through the clouds somewhere off to their right. She turned and followed her brother down the steps. It was slow going, because the steps were now slick with moisture and a curious green slime that they hadn't noticed when they were climbing them earlier that day.

'Maybe it's something to do with the tides,' Ally said quickly. 'Which means we must be close to the sea.'

Ken nodded, unconvinced. There was something about the steps which was puzzling him. They had gone another twenty steps before he finally voiced his opinion. 'Ally...Ally...don't you think these steps are getting narrower?'

'I thought I was imagining it,' she whispered. She looked down and measured the steps with her foot. They were definitely narrower than before. She was about to say something to her brother when they heard the footsteps ringing on the steps above their heads...

Paedur led Faolan down the narrow stone steps, hurrying to make the shelter and safety of the fog, while the arrows rained down behind them. The first arrow missed, hissing off over their heads. The second shattered on the steps behind Faolan, making him turn towards the sound. He actually saw the third arrow whistling directly towards him — when the bard's hook lashed out, its razor-sharp edge slicing the shaft in two. The fourth shot hissed off into the clouds, disappearing into the marshlands below.

'What'll we do if they follow us?' Faolan asked.

The bard shook his head. 'Their feet are too big for the steps,' he said with a grin. He also knew that there were no other exits off the stairs, so the Fomor would have to try to reach the bottom before they did. Paedur was hoping that they would reach the ground first so that they would be able to disappear into the Baddalaur Marshlands, where even the Fomor would have difficulty tracking them. It was only another few steps to the cloud...

Cold, grey-white fog swirled around his boots, beading them with moisture. It crept up his legs as he moved into the thick cloud. Feeling his way carefully now, unable to see his feet, he moved down another step, and another, Faolan's fingers digging painfully into his shoulder. Paedur glanced up at the golden-haired boy; he was twelve, three years younger than the apprentice bard, but the bard had packed more experiences into his fifteen years than most men did in their entire lifetimes. He smiled encouragingly at Faolan. 'We're safe now,' he started to say, and then bit off his words.

The Fomor Officer was leaning out through the window, the morning sunlight glinting off the metallic patch that covered his left eye. As the young bard watched, the Fomor lifted out a furry grey ball about the size of a man's head, and placed it on the top step. It lay quivering on the stone and then slowly a long slender leg unfolded from the furry ball. It was followed by a second... and a third...and then three more appeared in quick succession.

'What is it?' Faolan whispered, turning to look back up the steps.

'A damhan,' Paedur said quickly. 'Remember what I said about being safe..?'

Faolan started to nod his head.

'I was wrong.'

Paedur dragged Faolan along at a dangerously swift pace. The enveloping grey cloud was so thick that Faolan could barely make out the shape of the dark-haired boy in front of him. The clouds seemed to swallow all sound and the moisture was bitterly cold. They had run down about a hundred steps when they realised that the cloud cover was thinning. Faolan squeezed the bard's shoulder. 'Hold up a moment. Let me catch my breath.'

Paedur nodded. He seemed unaffected by the terrifying flight down the narrow steps.

Faolan jerked his thumb over his shoulder. 'What was that thing?'

The young bard squinted up into the cloud, and then tilted his head to one side, listening. 'It's a damhan. They resemble a large hairy spider, though their heads are larger and they have large pincers like a beetle. They originally started out as parasites on the Fomor, tiny spiders which fed on the ticks and fleas that live on the serpent folk.' He smiled coldly. 'But the Fomor bred them deliberately, growing them bigger and bigger. On the Fomor Islands in the south they're used to keep down rats and mice, and to keep the bird population in check.'

'Are they poisonous?'

'No; their venom will immobilise small creatures, and then

the damhan will devour them. But the manhunters are trained to attack the throat.'

'Manhunters?' Faolan breathed.

'They're trained to kill.'

'And that's what the Fomor sent after us?'

Paedur nodded.

'Then what are we standing around here for? Come on.'

They continued on down the steps. Faolan had lost his fear of falling; the fear of the damhan was greater. At every moment he expected to feel the giant hairy spider fall onto his neck and sink its pincers into his throat.

They had descended another hundred steps when they heard voices from below, muffled and made distant by the mist. The accent was peculiar, the language harsh and strange.

'Ally...Ally...don't you think these steps are getting narrower?'

There was a pause and then a female voice replied in the same peculiar accent.

'I thought I was imagining it.'

Paedur looked at Faolan and then reached down for the knife that he carried in the top of his right boot.

'Friends or foes?' Faolan asked.

'We're about to find out.'

*

Ken and Ally were shocked speechless when two boys, both wearing peculiar old-fashioned clothing, one with a spectacular-looking hook in place of his left hand and carrying a narrow-bladed knife, appeared out of the mist behind them.

Paedur and Faolan were equally shocked at the appearance of two humans, a male and female. It wasn't their clothes — although they were barbaric enough — but it was the colour of their fiery-red hair which amazed them. Only the Small Folk, the Fir Dearg, grew hair that colour, and yet these were too tall to be Small Folk. Faolan looked at Paedur as the red-haired boy stepped in front of the girl and raised a tiny-bladed knife.

'Who are you? What do you want?' Ken demanded, surprised to find that his voice didn't tremble too much.

The tall, dark-haired, dark-eyed boy with the curving hook stepped up to him, frowning slightly. He raised the hook and ran it down the side of his face, scratching his ear lobe thoughtfully.

He spoke softly in a strange lilting language.

'What did he say?' Ally demanded.

Ken shook his head. 'I don't recognise the language. It sounded something like Old Irish, or Scots Gaelic or maybe Welsh.'

'Were they the ones firing at us?'

'They're not carrying bows,' Ken said, 'and from the way the other guy keeps looking around, I'd say they were being chased.'

The boy with the hook slid his knife back into a sheath sewn inside his boot and pointed down the steps into the cloud. His narrow eyebrows raised in a silent question.

'I think he wants us to go,' Ken said.

'I don't think we should,' Ally murmured.

'I'd say we go. Whoever's chasing them was the person firing the arrows.'

'That's got nothing to do with us,' Ally said firmly. 'But where did they come from?' she demanded. She looked at the dark-haired boy. 'Who...are...you...?' she said loudly, pronouncing each word slowly.

He shook his head and smiled slightly. Pointing back up the steps, he made a disgusted face, baring his teeth, shaping his hand into a claw.

'He's trying to tell us what's up there,' Ken said slowly.

'He's trying to frighten us.'

'I'm frightened already,' Ken muttered. 'Ally, I think we should go.'

She nodded. 'We were going down anyway,' she said, turning away and beginning the slow and painful process of moving from step to step.

'Where have they come from? I thought this island was deserted.'

'It is,' Ally whispered, glancing back over her shoulder at the two strangers.

*

'They're human-kind, but strange,' Faolan said softly, even though he had a good idea that the strangers didn't speak his language. And yet that was impossible, because only one language was spoken across the De Danann Isle. There were numerous dialects and local accents, but entirely different languages were confined to the barbaric outposts or the great island to the extreme west, where the copper-skinned humans lived, or the enormous land mass to the east of the Isle where the black-skinned human-kind lived. These barbaric races had their own languages.

'And their clothing. The manufacture is peculiar, even the cloth is strange. And did you see their shoes?'

'Time for questions later,' Paedur said urgently. 'Remember the damhan.'

Faolan involuntarily glanced back over his shoulder. He was just in time to see the furry grey creature appear out of the mist.

Faolan's shouted warning brought them all to a stop.

The damhan was poised four steps behind him, on a level with his chest. The creature's long furry legs were tapping the stones, its pincers opening and closing with a clearly audible click.

'Don't move,' Paedur whispered. 'Its eyesight and sense of smell are poor; it tracks movement by disturbances in the air.'

'Ally,' Ken murmured, recognising the urgency in the dark-haired boy's whisper. 'Do you see it... ?'

'I see it. I just don't believe it...' She started to shake her head — and the creature immediately froze. Tiny blood-red eyes seemed to be looking in her direction.

Ken turned to look at his sister, but the sudden movement attracted the damhan's attention. It spat at its target. Ken felt a tiny spot of moisture on his forehead. Frowning, he touched it with his forefinger — and found there was a sticky thread from his forehead leading back to the enormous furry spider. He was reaching for the web when the damhan leapt!

One moment it was crouched on the steps, a quivering grey furry ball — and the next it was in mid-air, travelling along the almost invisible web, its legs splayed, its pincers wide.

Ken barely had time to scream before Paedur's hook flashed in an intricate figure-of-eight. The metal sickle sliced through the web both behind and in front of the creature and then, as it fell, neatly cut the damhan in half in an explosion of grey fur and thin green blood. Without a word, he nudged the remains of the creature off the edge of the step.

Ken raised a trembling hand to his forehead and peeled off the tacky web. He attempted to smile at the one-handed boy, but his entire face seemed frozen. He felt as if he were about to throw up. 'Thank...thank you,' he stuttered.

The dark-haired boy tilted his head to one side.

'Go raibh maith agat,' Ken tried in Irish, and this time the other boy frowned.

'Goran mathagan?' he said.

'I don't know what that means, but if it means 'Thank you,' then, yes, "Goran mathagan." '

'What did he say?' Faolan asked.

Paedur shook his head. 'I'm not sure, but I think they can speak some corrupt form of the language.'

Ken turned to his sister. 'I think they're speaking some ancient form of Irish.'

The one-handed boy tapped Ken on the shoulder and pointed down the steps.

'He wants us to go down,' Ken said quickly.

'I don't think we've any choice,' Ally whispered. She looked at the spider's green blood dripping from the dark-haired boy's hook, and suddenly realised that she was very frightened. Something was very, very wrong. She reached out and rested her hand on Ken's shoulder, following him down the steps.

*

They became aware that the mist was thinning about the same time they realised the temperature was rising. Ken saw the trees first, but he said nothing: towering, thick-boled trees did not belong on Skellig Michael. And there was always the chance that he was dreaming. He realised his sister had seen them when her fingers tightened painfully on his shoulder.

'Ken...?' she began.

'I see them.'

'But Ken...'

'I know.'

The trees appeared out of the mist. Immensely tall with enormous trunks, they towered up into the clouds, their branches trailing long beards of moss. Tiny, brilliantly-coloured flowers were scattered in the branches, and purple vines were wrapped thickly about the branches and trunks.

Brother and sister breathed deeply. The air was warm and moist, rich with the odours of growth and decay, sweet with unusual perfumes, bitter with what might have been animal or bird droppings.

Another dozen steps brought them out of the clouds. They stepped off the stone steps onto soft, springy earth.

'Where are we?' Ally breathed, her heart pounding painfully in her chest.

'Not on Skellig Michael, that's for sure,' Ken whispered.

They were looking out over a marshland. The trees they'd seen were clustered on tiny reed-covered islands, while between the islands, slimy water bubbled and swirled sluggishly.

The dark-haired boy stood in front of them both. He spoke slowly and distinctly to Ken, the words lilting and musical, ending on a note which seemed to indicate that he might have been asking a question.

Ken looked at Ally and they both shook their heads.

The boy with the hook lifted his right hand and cupped Ken's face, his long fingers just touching the cheekbones, resting against the ears, his thumb across Ken's lips. Lifting his left arm, he pressed the glittering hook against the left side of the boy's face. The metal was cool, tingling.

The one-handed boy spoke, and Ken winced; the hook seemed to be growing warmer, and there was a buzzing in his ears, a tickling deep in his throat.

'*Digante naois*...and you should be able to understand me now.'

The buzzing dissolved into words. Ken looked at him in wonder. 'I can understand you!'

'Of course.' He sounded almost surprised at Ken's amazement. He turned to Ally, who was watching him fearfully. She had seen what he'd done to her brother, and while he seemed to be unharmed, he was now speaking in the language of the two strangers. Taking a deep breath, she allowed the young man to place his hand against her face. His flesh was warm, and she could feel the hard skin along his fingertips and thumb. She winced when the hook touched her face. It might have been her imagination, but she thought she had seen curling letters cut into the side of the metal. They looked as if they were glowing as they approached her face.

'*Paedur sanamdam*...my name is Paedur. I am an apprentice bard,' he smiled. 'This is Faolan.'

'Where are we?' Ally demanded. She was *thinking* in English, but the words were coming out in this curious language.

'Introductions first, then explanations,' Paedur smiled again. 'You are strangers I see, lost, confused too,' he added, looking at them both.

'I am Kenneth...Ken, and this is my sister Alison, Ally for short. Can you tell us where we are? Something very strange has happened.'

The bard indicated his surroundings with a sweep of his hooked arm. 'These are the Baddalaur Marshlands...' He continued more slowly, when he realised that the strange pair didn't recognise the name. 'Falias the capital is to the south, Finias to the East, Gorias to the West and Murias in the North.'

Ken shook his head slowly. 'The names sound almost familiar...'

'These are the De Danann Isles,' the young bard continued, and then nodded as he saw comprehension dawning in the boy's eyes.

Ken turned to his sister. 'These are the De Danann Isles,' he said, barely able to contain his excitement. Ally shook her head stubbornly. 'This is Skellig Michael.'

The second boy, Faolan, suddenly grabbed Ken and Ally by the arm. 'We can talk about this later,' he snapped.

Ally shook her arm free. 'What's the rush? I'm going nowhere!'

Faolan roughly spun her around and pointed.

Splashing through the filthy water was a giant lizard, something that resembled a cross between a serpent and a crocodile. It was wearing armour and carrying a huge sword. There were two more behind it, carrying longbows that were as tall as themselves.

'Fomor,' Faolan gasped.

The serpent opened its mouth and screamed aloud. 'Stop. There is no escape!'

'This way,' Paedur snapped, turning and darting off into the marshland. 'Follow me.'

'Follow me. Step exactly where I step,' Paedur said loudly, his eyes fixed on the ground. 'If you miss the path, you'll be sucked down.'

Ally and Ken followed the bard without a word, while Faolan took up the rear, all staring intently at the ground, looking for traces of the path which only Paedur could see.

The ground was soft and spongy underfoot, foul-smelling liquid washing in over their shoes with every step. Neither Paedur nor Faolan who wore knee-high boots seemed concerned, but the sludge clung to Ally's sneakers and Ken's prized Doc Marten's were coated in green slime.

The bard led them up onto a small hillock that was crowned by an enormous and obviously ancient oak tree. This tiny island in the middle of the marsh was home to countless thousands of insects which immediately attacked the humans who had dared to invade their domain.

'Bugs,' Ally shouted, shaking her hands before her face. The insects were everywhere, hanging in the air like a fine mist. 'I'm not staying here...' she began, standing up. An arrow whistled into the tree by her head, vibrating like an angry bee. She stared at it in shocked surprise, before dropping to her hands and knees and scrambling around to the far side of the gnarled tree.

An arrow bit deeply into the ground inches from Ken's foot. He was amazed to find that it was nearly as tall as he was.

'Behind the tree,' Paedur snapped. Ken didn't need to be told twice.

Two more arrows buzzed into the tree trunk on either side of the bard's head. He didn't even flinch. He reached down for Faolan who was just climbing up onto the hillock and hauled him up. He pushed him around to the sheltered side of the tree as another arrow shattered off the tree trunk.

'We will be safe here for a while,' Paedur said, sinking to the ground, with the tree trunk at his back. He looked at his three companions, sizing them up. He realised he was probably the eldest at fifteen, the strange sister and brother looked about fourteen and thirteen perhaps, and he knew Faolan was twelve.

The long silence was broken when they all spoke together.

'What were those creatures?' Ken asked.

'Where are we?' Ally wanted to know.

'What do we do now?' Faolan said.

Paedur raised his hand, silencing them. He turned to Faolan. 'Why don't you tell Ally and Ken who you are? Some of this you may not understand, but I'll explain all later. It is their role in this affair that I do not understand,' he added.

'My parents are the Windlords,' Faolan began. 'They are the masters of the ancient wind-magic. The Emperor ordered them to reveal its secrets, but they refused. With my parents and sister, we were forced to flee the capital. The Emperor sent his personal Fomor guard after us. Their leader — the one they call the Officer — is an enormous beast with a metal patch over one eye.'

'Cichal,' Paedur said quietly. 'I've heard of him.'

Faolan looked at the brother and sister and jerked his thumb over his shoulder in the direction they'd just come. 'They raided Baddalaur just before dawn...' His voice trailed away and he turned to look at the bard. 'You spoke to me in my dreams. You warned me. How? Why?'

Paedur shrugged. 'I was in the observatory when the beasts came up through the sewers. I knew they could only be here for your family.' He touched the eye and triangle badge high on his left shoulder. 'Most people think this is a simple badge. But it can also be used to send thoughts and images across distances.

When a bard is telling a story, he can use the power of the badge to allow his audience to feel the emotion in the story he's telling.' He smiled slightly. 'I simply warned you that the beasts were coming.'

'But why?' Faolan wondered.

'Because you have to remain free. Balor the Emperor already knows too much. He needs only one piece of the ancient magic to make his knowledge complete: the Windlore. If he were to learn that, then he would control the world — and probably destroy it too.' He glanced at Ally and Ken. 'But I fear we are alarming our new friends. Please continue with your story.'

Faolan nodded. 'We escaped through the tunnels and into the library, but the Fomor caught up with us there. My father called up a wind within the central hall of the library and pushed the creatures back, but the effort was too much for him and he collapsed.' He dug his hands into his belt pouch and lifted out a small leather-bound book. 'Just before the beasts captured them, my mother gave me this and told me to go into the Northlands to bring it to my uncle Lugh, the last of the Windriders.'

'I know the legends of this Lugh Windrider,' the bard murmured. 'I didn't think he was still alive.'

Faolan lifted the book. 'My mother warned me that whatever happens, I've got to keep this book out of the hands of the Fomor and the Emperor — even if it means destroying it.'

Paedur stretched out his hand for the book. 'I am in my final year of training as a bard,' he said thoughtfully. 'I know most of the lore and legends of the De Danann Isle. I've heard of this book.' He turned it over in his hand. 'This is the Windlore, the collection of spells and magical lore that gives the rightful user the power over the element of the air.' He passed the book back to Faolan without opening it. 'Guard it well. All magic springs from the four branches of Elemental Magic: Earth, Water, Fire and Air. It is said that Air is the most powerful of the Elemental Magics,' he added. Looking up suddenly, he smiled. 'Aaah, Cichal has arrived.'

'How can you tell?' Faolan asked.

'I can smell him.'

The situation was disgraceful. Not only had the boy escaped, but several of his troop had been injured. And if that wasn't bad enough, his pet damhan was missing, and that really upset him — he had owned that damhan since it had hatched; he had trained it himself.

Although the human whelp had been alone when he'd fled the library, he had somehow managed to pick up companions. Cichal had seen the one-handed youth wearing the badge of an apprentice bard himself, and now there were more. The archers had reported seeing two others, strangely clad and red-haired like the Small Folk.

But at least they had them now. They were trapped on a mound in the midst of the marshland. Around them lay nothing but treacherous bogland, sucking pits and quicksands, and as soon as they moved out of the cover of the tree, Cichal's archers would be able to pick them off. Already the thick, gnarled tree trunk was studded with tall arrows.

The Fomor Officer knelt to examine the ground. He knew there was a track from where he was standing over to the hillock, but he couldn't see it, and even if he could, he wasn't sure he would have risked any of his men on the path. The enormous weight of the Fomor might be enough to send them deep into the soggy ground.

'We could burn them out, Officer,' one of the archers suggested.

'Fool! These swamps give off inflammable gases; do you want the entire marshlands to go up in flames?' He turned his great head from side to side, his teeth locked together in frustration. He had two options: he needed to drive the human-kind away from the tree...or break down the tree! Cichal hissed a short laugh. 'Bring me the gunner,' he commanded.

*

'And the last thing you remember about your own world,' Faolan said looking at Ally and Ken, 'was when you were walking down these stone steps on this island called Skellig Michael. You walked into a cloud there...'

'And ended up here,' Ken finished. 'We've somehow gone back in time.'

Paedur leaned forward. 'Only the most powerful of magics would have been able to draw you back in time, but I don't see the reason for it. Who would want you?'

'Could it have happened by accident?' Ally asked.

'Unlikely,' Paedur said, 'only a very powerful piece of uncontrolled magic could have plucked you from your own age, and any magician powerful enough to work that sort of magic would know enough to take precautions.'

Faolan sat up excitedly. 'When my father called up the wind in the library, he did so without any preparation. The effort was too much for him and he collapsed.'

The bard nodded. 'That could be it; some of the spell might have gone wild. The Wind that Blows Through Time might well have dragged you back.'

'But how do we get forward again?' Ally said in a rush. This was a nightmare, a mad, terrifying nightmare which she desperately wanted to wake up from.

'Only Faolan's father has the power to generate the wind to send you home,' Paedur said gently.

Ally looked at her brother, seeing her own fear reflected in his face. 'So we're stuck here?'

The bard nodded. 'I'm afraid so. However, there are worse places you might be stuck.'

Ally looked around her. She was sitting in the middle of a swamp. Her clothes were ruined; there was goo in her shoes, filth in her hair, she was goodness knows how many thousands of miles in space and time from home, they had been chased by a giant spider, shot at and now there were huge serpent-people chasing her. 'Name one place worse than this,' she demanded.

But before the bard could reply, there was a tearing snap from the direction of the Fomor and then one of the branches above their heads cracked and fell into the mire, splashing them with warm, foul-smelling liquid.

Faolan leaned around the branch. 'They've got one of those stone-throwing tubes.'

'It's a thick metal tube that uses an explosive powder to shoot stone balls,' Paedur explained without moving his position.

'A gun,' Ken nodded. 'We have them in our time.'

There was another snapping explosion and the entire body of the tree shook as a stone struck it solidly before bouncing off into the marshland.

'Either he's trying to knock down the tree or he's trying to get us to run,' Paedur said quietly. 'But this tree will take a lot of punishment, and we've nowhere to run to.'

'But we can't stay here forever,' Faolan protested. 'They'll bring up humans, or send someone out in a raft to get us.'

The bard shook his head. 'They don't even have to do that. All they have to do is to keep us here until nightfall...'

Although he didn't really want to know the answer, Ken asked the question anyway. 'What happens at night?'

'I don't know.'

'What do you mean you "don't know"?'

Paedur shrugged. 'I would suspect that because these hillocks are the driest spots in the marshland, a lot of animals crawl up out of the mud or slither in off the reeds to rest here during the night. But I'm only guessing. I really don't know.'

'Why not?' Faolan asked. 'I thought bards knew just about everything.'

'I don't know because no-one has ever spent a night in the Baddalaur Marshlands and lived to tell the tale!'

The point of the bard's hook bit into the soft ground, tracing a map. 'We are here in the marshes to the north of Baddalaur. The marsh gradually gives way to the Northern Forests, and these in turn lead into the province of Thusal and the northern Ice-Fields.'

'How long a journey?' Faolan asked.

The bard shrugged. 'On foot, I don't know. Twenty days...thirty.'

'Thirty days,' Ally said in horror. 'But what about us? We can't stay here for thirty days!'

'My sister's right,' Ken said slowly. 'Our parents will be terribly concerned.'

'Your only hope lies with Faolan's father or possibly Lugh, his uncle,' Paedur said. 'They are the Windlords: only they can send you back to your own time.' He shrugged. 'You really don't have a choice.'

'Nevertheless, what Ken and Ally say is true: thirty days is too long,' Faolan said. 'We'll need to make it into the Northlands sooner than that.'

'Then we're going to need some transport,' the bard mused, tapping his bottom lip with his hook. His face suddenly lit up with a rare smile. 'Have you ever heard of the nathair?'

Faolan nodded slowly. 'The winged serpents...but I don't see... ' he continued slowly.

'They come from the land far to the west of here,' Paedur

explained to Ken and Ally, ignoring Faolan. 'There, the copper-skinned folk worship them as gods, and it is true that some of the nathair are incredibly powerful and intelligent. They are supposed to be related to the Fomor, but I think that is unlikely. Some of the Fomor however, especially Officers, have their own nathair...'

'Cichal,' Faolan said excitedly. 'He would be sure to have a nathair.'

'Can I ask a question?' Ken said patiently. Paedur and Faolan turned to look at him. 'This winged serpent,' he began, 'are we really talking about a snake with wings?'

'Well, it's not really a snake with wings,' Faolan said slowly.

Ken started to smile. He thought it had been a bit ridiculous...

'It's more like a scaled bird,' Paedur said. Ken swallowed hard. He hated snakes, and just the thought of a giant snake made him feel quite ill. He turned to look at his sister, but she was leaning with her back to the tree trunk, her eyes squeezed tightly shut, lips closed in a straight line. 'Ally...Ally... ?' He reached over to touch her shoulder and she opened her eyes with a start.

'I thought it was a dream,' she whispered. 'I was sure I was going to wake up, and we'd be back on Skellig Michael...and ...and it would be time to go...and...and...and...'

A sob caught at the back of her throat. 'This is a nightmare.' The bard reached over and rested his hook on her shoulder. 'This is no dream,' he said, his voice deadly serious, his coal-black eyes boring into hers. 'This is not your world, but this is real, and you must believe in it. You can be hurt in this world, you can die here.' He glanced at Faolan and continued, 'This is our world. We know its dangers...just as you know the dangers of your world. Here, you must do everything we say, follow our advice, and in that way you will be able to return to your own world safely some day. There is much that you will find strange and bizarre here: there is magic in this world, there are powerful mages and wizards, witches and sorcerers, strange beasts, wondrous creatures, deadly insects and equally deadly plants in this world. I'm not telling you this to frighten you,' he added, 'simply to warn you to take care. And you don't have to believe in magic for it to work. It works, and it can harm you. Do you understand what I am saying?' he said seriously. Ally nodded slowly. 'Do you?' he asked Ken. The red-haired boy nodded. Paedur smiled. 'Good! Now, let's see what we can do about getting away from these beasts.'

Faolan patted his pouch which held the Book of the Wind. 'If only I knew a little of my family's magic, I'd be able to drive them off.' The bard started to nod and then stopped suddenly.

'Of course,' he murmured, 'how stupid of me.'

'What's wrong?' Faolan asked.

Paedur shook his head. 'Sometimes I think I'll never be a proper bard.'

Ken frowned. 'Why?'

Paedur stretched up his left arm and used his hook to catch one of the branches.

'Because bards are taught to think...and I haven't been thinking very clearly lately.'

He pulled himself up by his hook, until he could peer through the branches at the Fomor, but remain unseen.

Six of the serpent-folk including Cichal were standing at the edge of the marshland. One of the beasts was probing the depth of the water with a long spear, while two archers stood guard, watching the tree intently. A long grey-barrelled gun had been set up on the soft ground before them. It was in the process of being reloaded for another shot. As he watched, the gun belched smoke and flame and a round stone dug a deep hole in the muck at the base of the tree, spattering mud everywhere. The bard dropped back to the ground again. He had seen enough.

'I have a plan,' he announced. 'Ally, can you climb?'

Surprised, she nodded.

'Good. I want you to climb up into the tree and keep me informed. Tell me everything that happens — no matter how trivial.' He then looked at Faolan and Ken. 'I'm going to work a little magic, but I'm going to need your help. Help Ally up into the tree first. Make sure she can see, but cannot be seen.'

Faolan laced his fingers together and helped Ally scramble up into the tree, and then boosted Ken up beside her. She was behind a thick web of branches and leaves and while she could see clearly, she was invisible. Brother and sister looked at the serpent-folk, seeing them clearly for the first time. Ken shuddered. Ally put her arm around his shoulder. They had never been good friends, and the terms spent apart in boarding schools had driven a further wedge between them. But now they were alone together in this strange and alien world. They had no-one else.

'Are we ever going to get out of here?' Ally asked.

'If Faolan's father brought us here, then he will be able to send us back,' Ken said firmly, trying to convince himself. 'At least that's what Paedur said.'

'And if he can't?'

'You heard the bard — this is a magic place. Magic and sorcery works here...whether or not you believe in it! We have to believe we can get home again. I believe it. Do you?' he asked.

'I do,' Ally lied.

Cichal swore as yet another shot fell short of the tree. He had thought that the weapon might be able to knock over the tree, but so far only three shots had actually struck the trunk, the rest had either fallen short or twisted off to one side.

It was some consolation though that the human-kind were trapped. They couldn't escape...nor could he send his men over to them. But he could wait. He had no choice: he couldn't return to the Emperor and tell him that a boy, a mere human-kind whelp, had managed to evade him.

His long-nailed claw dug into the neck of the Fomor who was working the stone gun. 'What is the matter with this accursed device?' he snarled. 'Why can you not manage to hit something as large as a tree?'

'It is a matter of finding the range, and then gauging the amount of explosive powder to fire the charge across the distance.' The copper-scaled Fomor nodded at the stones scattered around the tree. 'We have not been using enough powder.'

'Use more,' Cichal snapped.

'Officer, I dare not...'

'Do it.'

'Put your hands on my shoulders,' Paedur said quietly. He was sitting cross-legged at the base of the tree, with his hook resting in the palm of his right hand. 'Many magicians started out as bards,' he explained. 'In the course of our training we learn a lot of simple magic spells, *petty magics* they're called. Now,' he continued, 'I want you both to think of an energy gathering in the pit of your stomach, flowing upwards through your arms, down into my body. You have to *believe* in this energy,' he added sternly, glancing up at Ken. 'Do you believe you can do it?'

'I do,' Ken said simply.

'Ally,' Paedur said softly, 'what is happening? Tell me everything.' Even as he was speaking, he closed his eyes and began to whisper the words of the ancient spell.

Ally wriggled forward on her stomach. Parting the leaves with the tips of her fingers, she began speaking softly and urgently.

'The Fomor are loading up their gun again. The one with the eye-patch is angry; he seems to be arguing with the gunner, he's pointing at the gun and a bag of what looks like black sand. He's making the other Fomor pour more of the black sand into the barrel of the gun. Eye-patch himself is going to fire the gun; he has a long glowing taper in his hand.

'Hang on. Something's wrong.

'All the Fomor are scratching. They're twisting, turning. Some of them are even pulling off pieces of their armour and scratching at their scales. Others are splashing water over themselves. They're in a frenzy...

'I can see something. A sort of black cloud gathering in the air above the serpent-folk. It looks like...yes, it is. It's a cloud of flies. The Fomor are being attacked by flies. The cloud is growing thicker. There must be hundreds of them. No, thousands. It's driving the Fomor crazy. Some of them are running away! Now they're all running.

'Only eye-patch remains.

'I can't see his head; it's covered in the flies.

'He's leaning towards the gun. It's pointing directly towards us. He's touched the taper to the fuse. It's started to burn...'

The gun exploded.

Too much explosive powder had been poured into the barrel of the weapon, and the tube burst. The force of the explosion lifted Cichal off his feet and sent him hurtling back into the swampy undergrowth. As he lay there dazed, he watched the golden-haired boy, the one-handed youth and the two red-haired humans scurry from their hiding place and pick their way across the swampy ground. They ran past the smouldering remains of the gun and then disappeared down along one of the trails that led back towards Baddalaur.

The huge Fomor war-lord lay back on the sodden ground and closed his yellow eye. Explaining this to the Emperor was not going to be easy. In fact, he wasn't sure he wanted to face the Emperor again until he had the boy.

He opened his single eye. He'd given orders for the captured Windlords to be sent back to Falias. He would continue to follow the boy. He had written a short note to the Emperor claiming that a magician had helped the boy to escape. He hadn't known how true it was when he'd been writing the note though: the one-handed whelp was obviously a magician. Those flies had not appeared purely by accident, and besides, Cichal's sense of smell had caught the faintly metallic odour of magic in the air. He didn't know what to make of the red-haired human-kind. None of the humans he'd met had red hair — except for the Cluricauns.

Maybe the Small Folk were involved in this; maybe they wanted the Windlords too. The Cluricauns and their cousins, the Fir Dearg, were both ambitious and dangerous. And their cunning was legendary.

Cichal's great claws tightened in the muck. These human-kind would regret that they had ever angered him. He had to bring the young Windlord back to the Emperor, but the other three whelps — aaah, maybe he'd cook himself a little feast when he caught up with them.

Cichal had trained to be a chef before he'd become a warrior.

*

Faolan and Ken half-carried Paedur across the swampland and down the narrow earth road. He was exhausted, practically asleep on his feet. Even with Faolan and Ken lending the bard their strength, the effort of calling the tiny flies to harass the Fomor had drained him. Ally moved ahead of the trio, watching out for the serpent-folk, but the pathway seemed to be deserted.

The track followed Baddalaur's high walls. They passed large barred holes in the side of the walls, which stank and dripped liquid filth into the marshland. Faolan was careful to give these pipes a wide berth. They carried sewer waste from Baddalaur, and bizarre creatures were rumoured to live in the pipes, feeding off the garbage.

Ally, who was about a dozen steps in the lead, abruptly held up her hand and then dropped flat to the ground. Without a word, Faolan and Ken followed her example, lowering the semi-conscious bard to the soft earth. While Ken remained with Paedur, Faolan crept forward beside Ally. She pointed ahead without saying a word.

About three paces ahead of her, the road dipped sharply into an almost circular hollow. To the left, there was an enormous sewer pipe set into the wall, dripping yellow sludge. The metal grill which usually covered the opening lay on the ground beneath it.

And gathered in the bottom of the hollow were five Fomor

standing around a creature out of legend.

'A nathair,' Faolan breathed.

The creature reminded Ally of pictures she'd seen of a pterodactyl, the great prehistoric flying lizards. The creature was huge, although the narrow head with its enormous beak, balanced by a bony crest that jutted backwards, seemed far too small for such a massive creature. There was a blindfold over its eyes. Huge paper-thin wings were neatly folded to its side. The nathair was covered in a grey leathery skin that was almost transparent in places, and Ally could clearly see a pulsating red blob in the centre of the creature's chest that marked its heart. She pointed to a curious wooden arrangement on the nathair's back.

Planting both elbows in the soft earth, Faolan cupped his chin in his hands. 'A saddle,' he explained. 'The crosses on the back are used for carrying supplies.'

She looked at the creature again. 'What did the bard mean when he said that we needed transport?' she asked, though she already had a very good idea of the answer.

Faolan turned to look at the nathair again and smiled. 'We'll ride out on the back of the nathair. We could be in the Northlands in a day...two days at the most.'

Ally turned from the winged serpent to look back at her brother: she knew that Ken hated snakes.

'But first we have to get past the Fomor,' Faolan continued. He glanced back over his shoulder at Paedur, but the apprentice bard was barely conscious. 'It's a pity the bard couldn't send some more flies to trouble them and drive them off.'

'Could we not frighten them off ourselves?' Ally wondered.

Faolan looked at her, a shy smile twisting his lips. 'These are Fomor,' he said softly, 'the most powerful, fearless warriors in the entire Seven Nations of the De Danann Isle. Nothing frightens them.'

'Flies did,' the red-haired girl reminded him.

Faolan nodded. 'Yes...yes they did, didn't they.'

*

Curoi heard the sound first. The Fomor warrior turned his head slightly, straining to catch the sound, his tongue darting, tasting the foul air. He hated this marshland. The stench was incredible, he could feel it coating his tongue, deadening his sense of smell, and he was sure he'd reek of damp marshland for the next ten days. The first thing he was going to do when he got back to Falias was to have a long, slow sand-bath. It would also help to wash off some of the countless tiny flies that had crawled in under his scales and were driving him mad.

There!

He heard the sound again. And was it his imagination or did the air taste even more foul than usual? He turned to look back along the path...and spotted the flies.

An enormous ball of the tiny creatures buzzed and circled in the air, and it was growing every moment.

Curoi opened his mouth to cry out a warning and then snapped it shut again, terrified that some of the tiny creatures might fly down his throat and lay their eggs inside him. He tapped the Fomor beside him on the shoulder and pointed up the track. The warrior hissed in alarm, and promptly snapped his mouth shut.

The five Fomor warriors looked at one another — and then they turned and ran. They were afraid of no human-kind, no beast or warrior, neither creature nor spirit...but they feared the tiny marshflies. These minute creatures laid their eggs on — and sometimes in — serpents. And the Fomor were serpents!

*

Ally was laughing so much she could scarcely stand. The plan had worked, the Fomor were running. She had been worried that the nathair would have been panicked by the flies too, but Faolan had pointed out that it was blindfold and couldn't see the swarm.

It had been a disgusting plan — quite disgusting. Revolting in fact. And her brother had refused to help. He was looking after the bard, he claimed.

Ally and Faolan had run back to the nearest sewer outlet. Using the broad flat leaves of a lily-like plant, they had scooped up some of the filth that dripped from the opening, and carried it back to the point where the path dipped downwards. It had taken several journeys for the two of them to gather enough leaves to attract the flies. They were both filthy and foul-smelling. Ally had attempted to wash her hands in a pool, but had only succeeded in smearing the dirt up her arms to her elbows. She was convinced she'd never smell clean again.

But when the flies had gathered in dozens and then hundreds and then thousands...and the Fomor had run, it had all been worthwhile. Ken helped Paedur to his feet. The bard's close-cropped black hair was plastered tightly to his head and he was still trembling slightly from the effort of calling the flies.

'Does all magic affect you this way?' Ken asked.

'What I did — calling the flies — would not have affected a trained magician in the slightest. But even the most powerful magician will take days to prepare and then recover from a major piece of magic.'

'I've always thought that magic was easy.'

'Nothing worthwhile is ever easy,' Paedur said slowly. 'If something is worth having, it's worth working for, worth paying a price.' He stopped, realising that the red-haired boy wasn't looking at him. Turning his head on stiff neck muscles, Paedur looked down into the hollow.

'Aaah, the nathair,' he said quietly. 'Excellent. It should be able to carry us all without difficulty.'

Ken shook his head quickly. His mouth was dry and there was a fluttering in the pit of his stomach. 'I'm not getting on that thing...'

'My brother's afraid of snakes,' Ally said quietly.

'The Fomor didn't seem to bother him,' Faolan said mildly.

'They looked too much like humans — that looks like a snake,' Ken said firmly. 'I'm not getting on that...'

Paedur turned to look at the boy, his large, dark eyes boring into him. He touched the bardic badge on his shoulder, and then spoke slowly and distinctly. 'You will come with me, Ken. You will not fear the nathair.'

Ken frowned, obviously confused. He started to shake his

head, but the bard continued, his voice smoothly controlled, 'You will come with me, Ken. You will not fear the nathair.'

Ken's eyes drooped and finally closed. He nodded. 'I will come with you. I will not fear the nathair,' he said in a monotonous whisper.

Ally looked at her brother in horror. He had been hypnotised by the bard.

'Now you know why bards are as highly prized as warriors in our land,' Faolan said simply.

Paedur turned to the nathair. Sensing the presence of the humans, it turned its long sinuous neck and hissed at them, showing a triple row of triangular teeth. A long, forked tongue lashed the air.

'What do we do now?' Ally asked.

A huge muddy figure crashed through the bushes, a long slate-grey sword clutched in a scaled claw. Cichal screamed at the four humans. They turned and ran towards the nathair without another word.

In his blind rage, Cichal blundered into the filthy leaves, disturbing clouds of flies. They swarmed up around the Fomor, covering his flesh in a moving shadow, sending him reeling backwards into some bushes. With his single eye squeezed tightly shut, unable to scream aloud his rage, all he could do was listen to the sound of the human whelps' laughter.

Faolan climbed up into the nathair's high-backed saddle, while Ally squeezed in behind him. He had ridden the nathair's smaller cousins back home, and knew how to control the temperamental creatures. Paedur helped Ken up onto the creature's back. The boy was silent and although his eyes were open, he looked and moved as if he were asleep. Paedur tied Ken's hands to one of the saddle supports to prevent him falling off. With a slash of his hook the bard cut the nathair free and climbed onto the creature's hard muscular back. Faolan twisted his head to look around at the bard.

'Which way is north?' he asked with a grin.

Paedur pointed to the right without a word.

'Can you control this thing?' Ally asked, peering over his shoulder.

'Of course,' Faolan said, with a confidence that he did not feel.

The nathair was directed by a series of hoods and blinkers over the creature's sensitive eyes. It had been discovered in the distant past that the nathair always flew towards the strongest light source. But it was only in the last few seasons that one of the Emperor's bards who specialised in animal lore had discovered that the nathair were hatched in caves: naturally their instincts would be to fly towards the light. By adjusting the hoods and blinkers over their eyes, it was possible to make the creature change direction, rise or fall, and even control its speed.

But it had been a long time since Faolan had ridden the small black nathair of his homeland...and he had never controlled a beast of this size. Taking a deep breath, he allowed light to come in through the top of the hood...

The nathair stirred, a shiver running down the length of its grey-scaled body. The tiny feet, that were used solely for support, stamped in the soft earth, and the enormous leathery, almost transparent wings unfolded. Its long narrow beak opened wide and then snapped shut.

Faolan lowered the eye covers a fraction more, allowing more light in.

The nathair's body coiled, twisting up tightly beneath it.

'Hang on,' Faolan commanded.

Even as he was speaking, the creature's serpent-like body uncoiled, snapping it upwards into the air. Its wings flapped, flapped and flapped again, attempting to catch a wind on which it could rise. It fell sickeningly and Ally screamed, but the fleshy wings suddenly filled with air and the serpent-creature rose upwards, twisting slightly in the warm air rising up off the marshlands.

They rose up through the chill damp clouds, past the ancient walls of Baddalaur, into the bright early morning sunlight. Ken was still staring straight ahead, under the bard's control, so only Ally was able to appreciate the splendid vista that appeared. Her first impression was that the De Danann Isle was green, as green as her native Ireland. Green fields and the darker green of forests covered the land, broken by bright silver-green threads that she guessed were rivers. There was a thin blue line on the horizon which she knew must be the sea and directly north, in the direction they were flying, snow-capped mountains rose into solid-looking white clouds.

Baddalaur fell away below them, an untidy huddle of stone and wood buildings surrounding a massive fortress-like building in the precise centre of the town. There were tiny insects scurrying around the town, gathering to look up at the serpent — and Ally realised with a shock that these were people. It was really only then that she realised how high they had risen. She felt her stomach lurch and her hands tightened around Faolan's waist.

'Don't worry,' he said, the wind snapping his words away, 'we won't be going too high.'

'How high can we go?' Ally wondered. The nathair's enormous wings were beating slowly and strongly, virtually silently.

'They prefer the higher altitudes where the wind gods are more powerful. The nathair ride the wind, gliding along the currents. Flying like this,' he nodded at the beating wings, 'is incredibly tiring for them.'

Ally rested her head on Faolan's shoulder, her long red curls mingling with his golden hair. 'Where are we going?' she said, speaking directly into his ear.

'Straight ahead,' he shouted, 'into the Northlands, beyond the Ice Fields of Thusal. We're looking for a village close to the Top of the World. My uncle is supposed to live there. I'll give him the Book of the Wind, and maybe he can use the magic to rescue my parents...and return you and your brother to your own time,' he added with a smile.

'And what happens if he cannot?' Ally asked fearfully.

Faolan shrugged. 'My father is the Windlord, he will be able to send you back to your own time.'

'And what happens if he cannot?' she persisted.

'He will,' Faolan insisted.

Ally nodded, unconvinced.

*

They flew on for most of the morning. As the day moved towards noon however, the nathair began to drift off course despite Faolan's efforts.

'The sunlight is confusing it,' Paedur shouted. 'Take it down.'

Faolan lowered the hoods over the creature's eyes, leaving only a slit at the bottom. The grey-skinned nathair began to spiral downwards. 'Have you any idea where we are?' he asked the bard.

Paedur, who had been stretched out on the creature's back, raised his head and looked around, attempting to gauge their location by the position of the sun and the direction of the winds. The ground below was rocky and broken, covered with enormous boulders and twisting streams and rivers, but with no obvious landmarks. The Ice Fields were far closer now, and the wind blowing towards them was bitterly cold, occasionally bringing flurries of snow and ice.

'We're into the province of Thusal certainly,' the bard said slowly, 'though I'm not exactly sure where. We should pass the Mion River soon, and at least one of the Seven Bastions of the North.'

'What are the Seven Bastions?' Ally asked, twisting in the saddle to look at him.

'They are seven fortresses built on this side of the Mion River,' Paedur answered her. 'They guard the Southlands from the savage Chopts and the Torc Allta.'

'There are many non-human races on the De Danann Isles,' Faolan continued, 'the Chopts are savage half-human, ape-like beasts. The Torc Allta are the Boar Folk. They are were-beasts, shape-changers.'

'Were-beasts?' Ally whispered, 'like werewolves?'

'Werewolves are the Madra Allta, the Wolf-Kind. Have you werewolves in your time?' he asked.

'Only in legends.'

'Every legend is founded on at least one grain of truth,' Paedur said suddenly. 'I think you will find that much of what is legend or myth in your own land began here, on the De Danann Isle.'

'The Tuatha De Danann were supposed to come to my land in the distant past. I thought it was just a folktale,' she said wonderingly.

The young bard grinned, showing snow-white teeth. 'Is this a myth, a folktale?'

With the ice-cold wind in her face, the sharp-sour smell of the nathair around her, the feel of the creature's uncomfortably hard body beneath her, Ally could only shake her head. This was no myth.

The nathair was close to the ground now, skimming above the boulders while Faolan looked for a place to land. They were in a rocky valley; what they had taken for low hills from above had turned out to be higher than they expected, with deep ravines and gorges sliced through them. Faolan guided the creature in between the broadest of two high walls of stone and glided silently down the long dark passage, heading towards the opening at the far end. There might be a place to land at the mouth of the ravine.

They burst out into bright sunshine and found they were facing a broad, glittering river. A golden-sanded beach bordered both sides of the river. Faolan brought the nathair into a smooth, soft landing, and immediately dropped the hood over the creature's eyes, blinding it. Its long narrow head immediately dropped. He waited until Paedur had lifted Ken off the back of the beast, and brought him back to consciousness with a snap of his fingers. Faolan then helped Ally to the ground. Faolan was preparing to dismount himself when he spotted movement in the rocks around them. He barely had time to shout a warning before the beasts attacked.

The creatures were enormous, standing easily as tall as the tallest man, covered in a thick coarse reddish hair. Their arms were unnaturally long. Deep-set tiny black eyes glared at the humans from beneath a thick ridge of bone. They were all carrying clubs and crude spears.

'Chopts,' Paedur breathed, turning slowly to count the creatures. There were seven of the huge beasts.

Ken winced as Ally's fingers bit into his shoulders. The creatures looked like apes and yet they were more man-like, and their weapons showed they had some skills.

The nathair suddenly shivered. Its huge wings spread, and its body tensed as it prepared to leap upwards.

'Faolan...' Ken shouted, but the nathair had already taken off, pushed high into the sky by its powerful muscles. The transparent wings spread, catching the wind, and it spiralled upwards.

'He's running away, leaving us,' Ally shouted, horrified.

The Chopts, who had scrambled away when the flying serpent had taken off, now closed in again.

Paedur pushed Ken and Ally towards the river. 'Run. I hope you can swim,' he shouted as they scrambled away. A Chopt struck at him with its spear; the bard's hook flashed out, cutting off the weapon's flint head. While the creature looked in astonishment at the broken spear, the bard turned and ran for the river.

With blood-curdling howls the Chopts raced after them.

Fear lent them speed. Ken glanced behind him once and saw that the creatures ran with a curious loping gait, their shoulders hunched, their knuckles occasionally brushing the ground. He was still confused; he clearly remembered standing in the steamy marshland at the foot of Baddalaur's walls looking at the huge nathair. What happened next was almost like a dream. He had been flying on the back of the serpent, cold air on his face, the ground tiny, far, far below. Now he was awake again, the marshland was gone, and he was being chased by savage-looking beasts.

'We're not going to make it,' he panted as the bard came alongside.

Paedur grunted. 'We'll find a place to stand and fight, maybe your sister will escape. The Chopts can swim — but badly. If we can hold them on this side of the river, she should be able to get away.'

'I've nothing to fight with,' Ken said, his mouth suddenly dry.

'There are plenty of stones,' Paedur said quickly. He pointed with his right hand to an enormous boulder. 'We can put our backs to that.'

The Chopts were confused when they saw two of their quarry running off to one side, while the third continued on straight ahead, towards the river. Five of the beasts came towards Ken and Paedur, while the remaining two continued after Ally.

Ken reached down and lifted a fist-sized lump of rock. He saw the bard pull a long-bladed knife out of his high boot, bringing his left arm up at the same time. The hook that took the place of his hand glittered in the sunlight.

The five Chopts stopped and looked at the two humans. The creatures were accustomed to their prey running away; few beasts had the courage or the strength to face them and fight. They saw their quarry open their mouths and show their teeth: the Chopts understood this sign, it was a sign of anger, rage, fear. They didn't realise that both Ken and Paedur were smiling.

The two humans had seen the huge winged shape drop silently down out of the sky behind the Chopts.

Faolan had returned.

He brought the nathair in low and fast, the tips of its wings almost touching the ground, dust swirling in behind. He rode the creature right into the midst of the Chopts, bringing them all crashing to the ground in a tangle of fur and grey scaled serpent. The nathair struck out at the Chopts, beating at them with its lashing tail and taloned wings, its long serpent's head snapping at them, its forked tongue stinging their bare flesh. Faolan dropped to the ground and, dodging both the Chopts and the nathair, ran to Paedur and Ken. 'I saw two more chasing Ally,' he panted.

Without another word, they turned and ran towards the river.

*

Ally had always hated sports in school. She used every excuse to miss the class, and she liked to pretend that she didn't need exercise. She was one of those people who seemed to be naturally healthy: her hair always looked shining, her skin was clear and she never seemed to put on any weight, no matter how much or how badly she ate. She always had this idea at the back of her mind that she was fit.

She was discovering now that she wasn't.

There was a stitch in her side that stabbed like a red-hot dagger with every breath she took, her throat was raw and her eyes and nose were both running. She was afraid she was going to be sick. She knew the Chopts were close; she didn't know how close because she was afraid to look over her shoulder, but she could hear their panting grunts growing louder, and actually smell their musty, vaguely unpleasant odour. She knew she had to reach the river...but even if she reached the river would she have the strength left to swim across it?

The rocky ground sloped downwards towards the river, the rough stones and grit gradually giving away to soft, shifting sand. Ally stumbled when she ran onto the beach, the sands seeming to clutch at her feet. She staggered on for a dozen more steps before she actually fell, the tips of her fingers splashing into the river's icy water. Behind her the beasts howled in triumph.

*

'They've got her,' Ken wailed as they raced towards the beasts. It was obvious that they were not going to get to his sister before the Chopts did.

'Not yet,' the bard said tightly. 'Give me the stone.'

Ken looked at him blankly before he realised he was still holding the stone he'd picked up earlier.

'Have you any firestones left?' Paedur asked Faolan.

The young man rummaged in his belt pouch, coming out with a small blue egg-like stone, which the bard snatched from his fingers.

Paedur stopped so suddenly that both Faolan and Ken ran on before they realised what was happening. By the time they returned to the bard, he was kneeling on the ground, with the little firestone positioned on the rock he'd taken from Ken. As they watched, he cracked open the little stone with the edge of his hook. A thick gooey paste spread over the stone. In one smooth movement, Paedur caught it with his hook and flung it towards the Chopts. The stone burst into a ball of flame in mid-air as the firestone paste ignited.

'You'll never hit them...' Ken began.

The blazing stone rolled between the feet of the two Chopts.

'...at this distance.' The sudden appearance of the blazing rock terrified the hairy beasts. The Chopts had a crude language and mythology and they knew what happened when hair caught fire. Fire was magical, mystical and deadly. They turned and ran.

By the time, Paedur, Faolan and Ken came running up, Ally was just climbing to her feet, her fear now turned to anger. She shook sand out of her hair. 'And where were you lot?' she demanded. 'I could have been eaten. I could have been killed. I could have been eaten and killed...or even killed and eaten.'

Without a word, Ken and Faolan grabbed an arm apiece and dragged the girl into the ice-cold waters of the Mion River, following the bard. Her cries finished in a high-pitched shriek.

Cichal leaned over the shallow bowl. It had been filled to the brim with water, and its surface now trembled and shivered with every movement in the cold, bare room.

'Well?' he hissed.

The room's only other occupant, an aged Fomor magician, silently raised a long-nailed claw and then pointed into the bowl.

Controlling his breathing with difficulty, Cichal leaned over the bowl and stared into the water. For a moment he saw nothing but his own distorted reflection in the water...and then, abruptly, the liquid clouded and cleared, and he found he was looking at the four human-kind sitting around a small fire. They seemed to be in a cave of some sort...and yessssss...the golden-haired whelp was looking at a book. The book. The Book of the Wind.

Cichal had to have that book.

Cichal *would* have that book.

The Fomor warrior concentrated on the image beyond the cave, trying to work out some clue to the human-kind's where-abouts. He saw low stunted trees and bushes, a rocky landscape, and just the barest thread of a river. He was shaking his head, about to turn away in disappointment when he noticed the colours twisting and curling across the night sky.

The Northern Lights!

He knew where they were now — or at least where they were heading. This time they would not escape — he swore it!

*

Ken and Ally sat quietly together, watching the bard tend a low fire. Faolan sat in the mouth of the cave, slowly reading through the first pages of the Book of the Wind, memorising the ancient lines of poetry. He was determined that even if the book were lost, then the information it contained wouldn't be lost with it.

Stars glittered in the skies although it was still only late in the afternoon. It was dark inside the cave, and the light from the small fire only served to make the shadows seem deeper, darker. The firelight ran along the bard's hook, turning it a liquid gold, and the shadows dancing across his face made him look old and tired.

'You'll like this,' Paedur said, glancing up at Ken and Ally.

They looked at him, unconvinced.

When they had swum the river, fleeing the Chopts, they had fled into the rocky wasteland, following the bard. They had run until their clothes were almost dry and both brother and sister were reeling from exhaustion.

Faolan had spotted the cave, and together he and Paedur had half-carried their two companions up into the cool darkness. The cave smelt fresh and although there were the ancient bones of some bird piled up in a corner, there was nothing to indicate that the cave was being used at the moment. While Ken and Ally rested, Faolan had started up a fire with flint and tinder and Paedur had gone out to find some food. He had returned with what looked like two dead hedgehogs and some large flat mushrooms. Ken had turned away in disgust, his hand pressed to his mouth, but Ally had watched fascinated as the bard had made a paste of mud and water and rolled the two spine-covered creatures in it, making a solid ball of mud. With his hook he scraped a shallow hole in the earth and dropped the hardened mud-balls into it and then built up the fire on top of it.

When the first faint odours of cooking meat drifted around the cave, both children's stomachs rumbled.

'I'm starving,' Ken muttered. 'It seems like ages since our last meal.'

'It has been,' Ally smiled. 'But since we're in the past, that means we had our last meal in the future.' She shook her head, puzzled.

'All my stomach knows is that it's been a long time since there was any food in it!'

'You'll like this,' Paedur repeated with a smile. He hooked the two hardened balls of mud out of the centre of the fire and cracked them open. The hedgehogs' hard, spiny skin came off with the mud and the smell of cooked meat was delicious. He served them thin slices of meat on mushroom plates. After the first careful bites, they wolfed down the remainder.

Paedur carried two slabs of mushroom to the cave mouth. He passed one to Faolan and sat down facing him, his back to the rough stone.

They ate in silence for a few moments, and then Faolan looked up at the bard.

'I haven't really had a chance to thank you...' he began.

'You've nothing to thank me for,' Paedur said softly.

'You saved my life, at least twice. Lucky for me you were there.'

The bard turned his head to study the rocky landscape. 'There is no such thing as luck. I was meant to be there at that time; the gods ordained it.'

Faolan nodded uncomfortably. He wasn't sure he believed in the gods and goddesses that the De Danann worshipped. Paedur looked up sharply, sensing something wrong.

'Do the gods really exist?' Faolan asked quietly.

The bard looked astonished. 'Of course. Why, surely you, of all people, believe in the gods. Your family are the Windlords, the most powerful magicians on the De Danann Isle.'

'I can accept magic; magic is just another part of the natural world. But I don't see where the gods come into it,' Faolan said stubbornly.

The bard shook his head quickly, a short angry movement. 'The gods and goddesses keep order in our world. I was in that room in Baddalaur today because the gods ordained it; they wanted us to meet and make this journey northwards.' He turned to look at the red-haired brother and sister. They were lying down at the back of the cave, the girl curled in a tight ball, the boy flat on his back, snoring gently. 'It was no accident that pulled these two back through time; the gods decided it. They're here for a purpose.' Anger made the young bard's voice cold and hard. 'We are the Tuatha De Danann, the People of Danann, worshippers of the goddess Danu. She saved you today, she brought you safely through the marshland, brought us to the nathair, carried us here, saved us from the Chopts. Would you have managed all this on your own? No,' he shook his head firmly. 'No, because without the goddess's help, you wouldn't have made it outside of Baddalaur's walls!' The bard strode out into the gathering night.

Faolan finished the rest of his meal, although he didn't have much appetite left now. Maybe what the bard had said was true, but Faolan found it hard to accept the existence of the many gods and goddesses that the Tuatha De Danann worshipped. Maybe there was some truth in what the bard had said though. Faolan picked up the Book of the Wind again and turned it around and around in his hands. He had certainly been extraordinarily lucky to escape with the book and make it this far northwards without being captured. Maybe luck had nothing to do with it: maybe there was a god or gods.

Moving away from the cave mouth, he slid the book back into his pouch and curled up on the dry earth. He was exhausted, every muscle aching, his head beginning to pound. But before he finally fell asleep, he whispered a prayer of thanks to the goddess Danu.

Moments later, Paedur returned to the cave. He was a little ashamed of his outburst, but he had trained for long enough to know that the gods relied on the worship of men. '*Faith lends substance,*' was the motto of the Old Faith. It meant that the more people who worshipped the gods, the stronger they became. When men no longer worshipped a god, that god faded away: he 'died of starvation'.

Paedur stood in the cave mouth, looking over the trio. He wondered about the brother and sister from the Time to Come.

Why were they here? They were more of a liability than a help: they needed constant looking after. He shook his head; obviously the goddess had some use for them. They had adapted well though, accepted what must seem very strange and bizarre indeed.

Paedur settled himself into the mouth of the cave, his long legs stretched across the opening, his knife by his right hand. Anything coming into the cave would have to cross him. He closed his eyes as a huge yawn made him fill his lungs with cold night air, and then settled himself for sleep.

Ally, who had been watching the bard through half-closed eyes, finally allowed sleep to claim her when she saw Paedur take up his position across the door. She trusted the bard. She felt safe in his presence.

It seemed that only moments had passed before they all awoke to the sounds of high-pitched terrified screaming.

'Banshee!' Faolan said, his voice sounding shaky.

'Not a banshee,' Paedur said firmly. 'I've heard a banshee cry — it's not a sound you ever forget,' he added grimly.

Faolan turned to Ken and Ally. 'A banshee is....'

Ken nodded, interrupting him. 'We know: a supernatural woman whose cry warns of death,' he said quickly.

'People in Ireland still claim that they hear the banshee,' Ally added.

They were both surprised when Faolan shook his head. 'There is nothing supernatural about the banshee. They are very real indeed. It is a tribe composed entirely of women; no men have ever been seen. Some people claim that they are half-human, or related to one of the beast-folk, but no-one really knows. They live deep in the ground, emerging only to kill. They are snow-white because they rarely see the sun: white hair, white skin, blazing red eyes. Their scream is designed to paralyse and stun their prey.'

'What happens to their prey?' Ken asked, not sure if he really wanted to know.

Faolan shrugged. 'No-one knows.'

'They're vampires,' Paedur said, without turning around.

The scream ripped through the night again, silencing them. The bard tilted his head to one side, listening. Ally tapped him on the shoulder and pointed to the left. 'It came from over there.'

Paedur nodded. 'That's what I thought.'

'It sounds like an animal,' she continued thoughtfully. The sound was vaguely familiar.

'You stay here,' Paedur commanded, 'I will investigate.'

'We'll stick together,' Faolan said firmly, and both Ken and Ally nodded.

The bard looked at them and shrugged. 'As you wish. But let's stay close. We don't know what's out there.'

The bard led the way down the rocky path, picking his way carefully over the broken ground. Although it was close to midnight, the sky was brilliant with stars, and the shifting curtain of the Northern Lights curling across the sky helped provide a faint illumination. Ken found that with the exception of the Pole Star, the patterns were strange and unfamiliar. There was a shape that might have been the Plough, but it was twisted around the wrong way...and then he remembered that the stars weren't fixed in the heavens. He was looking at the stars as they would have been several thousand years ago. The boy shivered, abruptly realising just how far away from home he and Ally were.

He hadn't really thought too closely about his present predicament. There hadn't been time. Everything had seemed to move so fast, it was almost like a dream...or a nightmare: huge spiders, snake-people, flying serpents, a one-handed boy, a magician's son, ape-like beasts, magic. Yes — it was a dream, he was convinced of it now. But if it was a dream, then why was he so cold, how come he could feel the wind plucking at his skin through the slits he'd cut in his jeans, and how could he feel the sharp stones beneath his shoes? Could a dream be that vivid?

The scream bit through the night again, and the bard stopped so suddenly that Ken walked into him, making the older boy hiss in annoyance. He raised his hand for silence, his head turning from side to side, trying to track the scream. Unfortunately the rocks surrounding them echoed and re-echoed the sound, bouncing it from rock to rock, making it virtually impossible to position it accurately.

'Over there, I think,' Ally said slowly.

Paedur nodded. 'I agree.'

Faolan stepped up to the bard. His small knife was in his hand and he kept looking around nervously. 'What about Chopts?' he asked.

'They don't fight at night. They believe that if they die away from their own camp, then their gods will not see their souls leaving their body, and they will be doomed to walk this earth as spirits.'

Faolan laughed shakily.

'Don't laugh,' Paedur said sharply. 'Things walk the Northlands that have never been explained. Have you never heard of the Ice-Wraiths?'

But before Faolan could answer, the high-pitched scream came again, this time sounding very close indeed.

'It sounds like an animal,' Ally murmured, stepping forward, moving towards the sound.

'Ally,' Paedur warned.

The girl was turning towards him when she disappeared with a crash, a cloud of dust swirling up marking her position. Her screams joined the animal's howling.

Ken would have run to her, but Faolan grabbed him by the arms, holding him while Paedur stepped cautiously forward. 'It's a trap,' Faolan said urgently, 'she's fallen into an animal pit.'

Ken was shocked speechless. His sister was trapped in a pit with some beast. He watched as the bard dropped to the ground and crawled forward to the edge of the large hole that had opened up in the ground. He thought he was going to throw up when he suddenly realised that she'd stopped screaming — and so had the beast. Ken heard the bard call out to her, and sudden tears sprang to his eyes when he heard her reply.

'Ally...Ally...Are you all right!'

'Of course I'm not all right!' Her voice echoed slightly off the stones. 'I've torn my jeans, I've scraped my hands and I'm bruised all over.'

Paedur looked back over his shoulder. 'She's all right,' he grinned.

'The animal,' Ken said quickly. 'What's down there with her?'

Paedur leaned over the hole and looked down. When he looked back, there was a broad smile on his face.

'What is it?' Ken demanded.

'A pig,' Paedur said simply.

The pig was about the size of a large dog. It had unusually long legs and it was covered in a thick coat of coarse reddish-pink hair. Its eyes were a vivid pink, and two tusks curled up from its lower lip. A pattern of lines and jagged stripes had been etched into the tusks. It sat at the back of the cave and looked from person to person, although it kept staring at Ally, who had insisted they save it and had carried it up out of the pit herself.

Paedur, who had resumed his place at the mouth of the cave, nodded at the creature. 'The Chopts don't hunt at night, but they set their traps for the animals who do. Our little pink friend there would have ended up on some beast's dinner plate. More importantly however, it tells us that there must be a Chopt encampment around here somewhere. We should move now, before daylight, before they come out to check their traps. They'll be upset when they discover someone's stolen their dinner,' he added with a smile.

'But what do we do with the pig?' Ally asked.

Paedur looked surprised. 'Nothing. It's a wild pig; it can fend for itself.' He nodded to the east. 'We had better move. It will be dawn soon.'

Ally reached over to stroke the pig's hairy back. The bristles were as stiff as a brush. It quivered slightly beneath her touch.

'Ally,' Ken said, standing in the mouth of the cave.

'Coming.'

The pig followed Ally out of the cave. She stood and looked back at it. 'Go away, go home. Shoo!'

It cocked its head sideways, looking at her.

'Off you go.'

'Ally,' Ken said urgently. 'The others are waiting.'

'But the pig is following me.'

'Let it follow you; it'll soon get tired.'

Ally turned for a last look at the pig and then she hurried out after her brother. The pig waited until she had vanished down the rocky path, before it trotted out of the cave after her.

Paedur was crouched down examining the track when Ken and Ally rejoined them. Faolan kept a nervous watch on their surroundings. In the grey half-light of the pre-dawn, broad vaguely human-like footprints were clearly visible. 'The Chopts use this track,' the bard said simply, 'so we have to be well away from it before they wake and check on their traps.'

'Can we not just cut across country?' Ken asked.

The bard shook his head. 'Look around you. We'd waste too much time climbing the rocks and crossing the ravines and crevasses. No, our best route is along this track — the only problem is that we're heading directly toward a Chopt encampment. Let's hope they sleep late.'

The track they were following led into a long narrow split in the high rocks. There was barely enough room for two people to walk side-by-side. The high walls kept the floor of the crevice in shadow and the chill wind that was funnelled through the opening made them all shiver.

'We'll have to see about getting us all some suitable clothing,' Paedur murmured.

'How?' Faolan asked, 'I've no gold, no silver. Have you?'

'Bards don't carry coin,' Paedur said softly. 'But don't worry: I'll pay for some food and clothing with a tale.'

Faolan couldn't hide the smile that crossed his face.

'It's not an idle boast,' Paedur said sharply. 'A bard does more than just tell stories. He keeps alive the history of our land, he brings gossip, tells which markets are looking for which produce, what goods are fetching the highest prices. Bards deal in information. In isolated parts of the country, information like this is especially valuable.'

'So all we have to do is to find a village,' Faolan said.

The bard shook his head. 'First we have to escape the Chopts.'

Even as Paedur mentioned their name, one of the huge hairy creatures dropped down into the ravine, ten steps in front of him. The beast opened its mouth, revealing long pointed teeth, and roared.

The Chopt moved forward slowly, an enormous club in its hairy paw. Its small red-rimmed eyes fixed on the young bard, marking him as the most dangerous because he held weapons in his hand.

'Run!' the bard said, without turning his head. 'Back up the ravine. I'll try to hold it here.'

'We'll throw stones at it,' Ken said quickly, 'you can run back while it's distracted.'

'Do it!' Paedur said quickly. He had his left arm up before him, his curved hook glittering in the light. He held his knife loosely in his right hand. He was wondering if he could use the bardic 'voice' on the creature.

He had been taught in Baddalaur that 'a trained voice is the most powerful of weapons,' and over the years he had perfected the ability to use his voice to make his listeners feel different emotions — love, fear, hate. He had also been taught to use the semi-magical 'three strains', a sing-song chant that induced incredible happiness, complete sorrow or a deep dreamless sleep upon whoever heard it. He wondered if he could use it on the Chopt. He opened his mouth to shout...when the small pink pig trotted between his legs.

The Chopt stopped as if it had been struck. It looked at the creature and then took two steps backwards.

The realisation of *what* the pig was struck the bard just as the first shafts of sunlight broke through the morning clouds and lit up the ravine.

Ally had run forward when the pig had slipped past her, but Ken had grabbed his sister, attempting to haul her back. Faolan had grabbed them both...and so they all saw the pig *change!*

A deep shudder ran through its body, its muscles visibly rippling beneath its skin, and the short reddish-pink hair that covered its back bristled. The pig grew.

Its legs thickened and lengthened, its body broadened, the chest deepening, stomach flattening. Its spine straightened, the hair on its back coarsened, matting its body like a second skin. It reared up on its hind legs, bones and muscles popping with a sound like breaking wood.

It became a man.

The broad round head turned to look at the four humans. The face had altered, shifted, giving it a more human-like appearance, but it was still unmistakably the face of a pig. The forehead was broad, the cheekbones prominent, the bright pink eyes were deeply sunk. The snout was still that of a pig and the two tusks that curled up from the lower lip almost came to the level of his eyes.

'Torc Allta,' Faolan breathed, 'boar-folk.' The boar folk were the most savage of the Were-Beasts. He looked past the Torc Allta to the Chopt: why, even it was frightened of the man-boar.

The Torc Allta bent its head to look at the humans. 'You have nothing to fear from me,' it said in a thick, muffled voice, grunting some of the syllables. It then turned away and faced the Chopt. The ape-like beast looked at the creature. It half-turned, as if it were about to walk away, but it suddenly shifted and sprang straight towards the man-boar, its club raised high.

The Torc Allta caught the descending club in both its v-shaped claws and wrenched it from the Chopt's grasp. It smashed the club off the rock wall with enough force to shatter the hardwood club into thousands of tiny splinters and pulverise part of the stone to white powder. With a high-pitched yelping scream, the Chopt turned and ran down the ravine. Tossing the stub of the club aside, the Torc Allta turned back to the humans.

'You have nothing to fear from me,' the Torc Allta repeated.

He lifted his head slightly, searching out Ally, who was standing behind her brother and Faolan, 'And you, copper-hair, I am in your debt.'

Paedur stepped up to the huge man-boar. Although the bard was fifteen summers old and tall for his age, the beast stood a head and more taller than him and was incredibly muscled. And yet the bard knew that this wasn't a fully grown Torc Allta.

'You saved our lives, Torc Allta,' he said gravely, 'we are in your debt.' He deliberately returned his knife to its sheath, realising that he was taking a risk, but his instincts told him that the beast would not harm them.

The man-boar nodded slightly. 'I am Ragallach na Torc Allta.'

'You are far from home, Torc Allta,' Paedur said.

'The Torc Allta have no home,' Ragallach grunted. 'But you are correct, we dislike this barren land — it reminds us of our homeland. I was travelling south to Falias with my family when we were attacked by a nathair. In the confusion, I was left behind, and I'm afraid I blundered into that trap.' His mouth split in a savage grin. 'It would have been interesting. I am still young, twelve summers as you measure time, so I cannot control the were-change. Every night when the sun dips below the horizon, I return to the pig-shape. With sunrise I assume this form.'

'But the Chopts do not hunt at night,' Paedur said nodding, realising what Ragallach was saying. 'They would not have been able to take you from the pit in your present form, while you would not have been able to escape while you were in the pig-shape.'

The man-boar nodded. 'And the sides were too steep, the mud was too soft for me to climb out. I would probably have died of starvation in the pit...unless the Chopts discovered some way of hastening my end.'

Still looking at the Torc Allta, Ken touched the bard's sleeve. 'We should be moving on, just in case that thing comes back with help.'

The Torc Allta nodded. 'That is possible. The beasts like to hunt in packs.' He pointed down the ravine. 'I will walk a little way with you, if I may. Perhaps my presence will frighten off the creatures.'

The bard bent his head to hide a smile. 'I'm sure it will.'

Ally walked alongside the Torc Allta. It was a terrifying — yet thrilling — experience. Ragallach was simply enormous, and yet, despite his bulk, he moved with a sinuous grace. He reminded her of the jungle cats she'd seen in the zoo. She found it impossible to work out how the small hairy pig she'd lifted out of the pit could turn into such a creature.

'Are you really only twelve years old...twelve summers?' she asked eventually.

Ragallach bent his head to look down at her. His mouth opened in a terrifying grin, revealing sharp pointed teeth. Whatever else he was, he was no vegetarian, she decided. 'I'll be thirteen this summer, copper-hair,' he said very softly, his voice sounding almost human, without the grunting snuffling sounds.

'Do you have a name?' he asked.

'Alison,' she said shyly, 'but everyone calls me Ally.'

'I shall call you *Al-ison, A-lission*, Alison,' he finally managed to say.

'Why did you save my life?' he asked suddenly.

Ally shrugged. 'I heard the sound of a creature in pain.'

'It could have been a trap.'

'I didn't think of that.'

'Then you must be a stranger to the De Danann Isles.'

'My brother and I were pulled back through time to this place.'

Ragallach glanced sharply at Paedur and Faolan. 'And now you walk with the hook-hand and the golden-hair. There is a tale here.'

'Faolan's family are the Windlords. We think his father's magic may have pulled us back through time. We're seeking his uncle in the Northlands. He is a Windlord; he knows the wind magic. We're hoping he can help us,' she said quickly.

The Torc Allta nodded. 'He will,' he grunted. 'And where is golden-hair's uncle?'

'In the Northlands, beyond the Ice-Fields of Thusal, in a village close to the Top of the World.'

'A place of great danger,' Ragallach mumbled.

Ally nodded. 'I'm frightened.'

The Torc Allta gently placed his huge v-shaped hoof on her shoulder. The broad nails looked as if they were carved from stone. 'You have nothing to fear, copper-hair. I think I will walk with you until you find this Windlord.'

'But your family...' Ally began.

'I am a Torc Allta. I am twelve summers, soon to be thirteen. There comes a time when the child becomes an adult, a time when decisions are made. This is my time.'

Ally patted the hairy claw. Ragallach's presence was comforting. 'I don't know how to thank you...' she began.

'There is no need for thanks. This is something I want to do.'

*

The ravine opened out onto a broad rocky plain. The landscape was desolate, reminding Ken of pictures he'd seen of the moon. The ground was grey, covered with rough stones and pebbles, pitted with holes and craters, some of which held what looked like bubbling mud. Snow-capped mountains were clearly visible in the distance. The wind blowing towards them was bitterly cold, stinging exposed skin. Both Ally and Ken began to shiver, and even Faolan, who was more suitably dressed, wrapped both arms around his body, tucking his hands into his armpits. Only Paedur and Ragallach seemed unaffected.

'We need clothes for the copper-hairs and the yellow hair,' the Torc Allta grunted. He still had difficulty with human names.

Paedur nodded. 'We're going to need some food too. We'll have to find a village.' Shading his eyes with his hand, he stared out across the plain, squinting in the pale sunlight.

The Torc Allta squatted down on his haunches. His broad head was on a level with the bard's shoulders. Closing his eyes, he tilted his head back, his boar's snout wrinkling as he smelt the bitter air. His left arm rose, pointing north and west. Suddenly he surged to his feet, his eyes snapping open. 'Fire and blood. I can smell fire and blood.'

The four humans turned in the direction he was pointing. A pale grey plume of smoke curled up into the clear sky.

Paedur pointed with his hook. 'That's where we must go. We need food and clothes before we go any further.'

'But Ragallach said he smelt fire and blood,' Ken protested. 'That means a fight. We could be killed.'

'If we continue on into the Northlands without proper food and clothing, then you will surely die. The Torc Allta and I would survive, Faolan too possibly. But not you.' The young bard smiled his cold, ironic grin. 'We really don't have a choice.'

Cichal the Fomor had flown north with five of his Troop riding on three nathairs. It was risky keeping so many nathairs so close together. They were solitary creatures, only coming together once a year to breed, but the Fomor Officer was willing to balance the danger of the flying serpents fighting amongst themselves with his urgent need to capture the human-kind.

News of Faolan's and Paedur's escape had spread like wildfire through the entire town of Baddalaur, and somehow the message had got back to the Emperor himself. Cichal had a suspicion that one of his own men was a spy for Balor the Emperor.

The message that had come back from Balor was simple: bring back the boy and the book...or else. Cichal didn't want to know what the 'or else' was. The Fomor Officer feared nothing and no-one...except the Emperor, Balor. Neither Cichal nor his Troop wanted to travel into the icy Northlands. They were cold-blooded creatures; snow and ice were amongst their greatest enemies. A warm blooded human could live for days in the Northlands: a Fomor wouldn't last a day. However, they had no choice.

Cichal had spent some time in Baddalaur's enormous library, examining the maps of the De Danann Isle. Information about the Northlands was scarce. The province of Thusal was wild and unpopulated, the home of bandits and beasts, half-humans, were-creatures and wild magic. But why was the human whelp, Faolan, travelling northwards? And what about the young bard, why had he joined him?

Cichal had discovered a little about the bard from the college records: he was a brilliant student with an extraordinary memory and his tutors had already decided he had the makings of a Bard Master. Both his father and uncle had been Bard Masters before him; that meant he would know a lot of the ancient lore...and the ancient magic. And who were the two red-hairs, the curiously dressed male and female? How did they fit into this picture?

Cichal discovered a few villages scattered close to the Top of the World, on the charts. They were mostly inhabited by trappers and hunters. It seemed likely that the humans would head for one of these...but which one? Cichal's long talon scratched the thick parchment map as it traced a line from Baddalaur to the nearest northern village. Assuming the puny humans would need food, clothing or just rest before they continued their journey into the desolate Ice-Fields, they would stop at a village...and the nearest village was here! Cichal's talon punctured the parchment.

Well, Cichal and the pick of his Troop would be waiting for them. Five Fomor and himself would be more than enough to take an insignificant human-kind village.

*

The village had no name. Situated on the very edge of the Thusal Ice-Fields it had no need of a name. It was the only village for a day's travel in any direction. It consisted of a dozen wood and stone huts, with turf roofs, clustered behind a fence of tall, pointed hardwood stakes. There was a deep pit both in front and behind the wooden fence. It was principally there to keep the beasts out and the villagers' own stock in and it provided some protection from the creatures that inhabited this wild land. The Chopts had learned long ago that there was no point in attacking the village: here the humans were just as savage as the beasts themselves. They had to be, to survive in the wild landscape. Their main trade was in furs, exotic woods and berries, and some precious stones that they scooped up out of the streams.

When the three flying serpents with their six hideous riders had dropped out of the sky into the centre of the village, the people hadn't panicked — as Cichal had expected them to do — instead they had calmly seen to their weapons and taken up defensive positions around the village.

The fight was brief and furious. Cichal and his Troop found themselves trapped in the centre of the village, while the humans closed in around them, raining spears, arrows and stones down on top of them.

Cichal didn't believe what was happening. This was obviously another bad-luck day. Perhaps his savage serpent-gods had deserted him. Maybe he needed to pray more often, offer bigger, more expensive sacrifices. First a single human whelp had managed to give him the slip and insult him before his Troop and the Emperor, and now this village of fur-clad savages were holding off the finest fighting force on the De Danann Isle.

As the humans closed in, Cichal took a flying leap and landed on the back of his nathair. The creature visibly sagged under the Fomor's great weight. Cichal urged it upwards. The nathair strained, its muscled body coiling, then abruptly propelling it upwards, its huge wings snapping out, hauling it up into the icy air.

Now Cichal had the advantage. The nathair were fighting creatures, trained to use their wingtips, teeth and tails in battle. The Fomor had the nathair circle down over the village, its armoured tail striking at the wooden huts, its wings battering the humans. Within a dozen heartbeats, it had demolished part of the village, and scattered the defenders. It was then an easy matter for the five remaining Fomor to round up the defenders and herd them into the centre of the village. In the background one of the huts blazed where its turf roof had caught fire.

When Cichal landed he was in a foul mood. He was even more disgusted when he discovered that the village's brave defenders had all been women: the men were in the Northlands, hunting.

He strode up to the first villager, a tall, dark-eyed women, her long black hair kept away from her eyes with a simple leather band. Although he was twice her height, the woman looked at him without flinching.

'I am Cichal, Officer of the Fomor. How dare you attack the Emperor's warriors...'

'When beasts on serpents fall out of the sky in the middle of the day, you assume they mean no good. You attack first, talk later.'

Cichal nodded. He could understand those reasons: maybe they shouldn't have dropped down into the middle of the village unannounced. 'In the name of Balor, Emperor of the De Danann Isle, I command you to assist me in the capture of a band of renegades.'

The woman looked up at him, and then she wrinkled her nose and coughed. 'You smell.'

The villagers gathered behind her howled with laughter.

Cichal hissed. 'You would be foolish to make an enemy of me, human-kind.'

The woman grinned, showing short stumpy teeth. 'You don't frighten me, serpent-folk. I have lived all my life in the North-lands, where I have seen all manner of truly terrifying creatures and beings: snow-cats, were-beasts, Ice-Wraiths, giant elks and Chopts. Some of them are even uglier than you.'

Cichal's teeth clicked together in astonishment and frustration. Usually the sight of a Fomor was enough to send any human scurrying for cover.

'Listen to me, human woman. There are four of your human-kind coming to this village soon. I want them. Assist me, and I will ensure that the Emperor gets to hear of it, and he will undoubtedly reward you. Hinder me however, and I shall be forced to burn your village to the ground. Now, give me your answer,' he snapped.

'We will not help you,' the woman said defiantly.

The Fomor hissed like steaming water. His threat to burn the village had been simple intimidation. He knew if he did that, then the smoke would rise up and darken the sky. It would be a visible warning that all was not well, and the four human-kind might well decide to avoid the village. 'Lock them up,' he commanded his Troop tiredly. 'Place a guard on the door. If anyone tries to escape, eat them!'

Cichal went to stand by the village gate, looking out across the barren countryside. The four human whelps would come this way — he was sure of it. And then he'd be able to head back to the capital where at least people were terrified of the Fomor and no-one would dare to question his power. It had been a long chase, but at least the end was in sight now. The Fomor shivered. Cichal was cold, tired — and hungry. Perhaps he *would* burn this village once he had captured the whelps. Maybe he'd reward his Troop by allowing them to roast a few of the human-kind over the fires before they returned to Falias. Cichal's teeth sparkled in the dying light. He thought of the woman who had defied him — and laughed. The Fomor glanced up into the sky, gauging the time by the position of the sun. Night came early to the North-lands, and stars were already beginning to sparkle in the heavens. He wondered where the human-kind were.

The village women had been gathered together in the Council Room, a long, narrow building in the centre of the village. There was only one door into the tall windowless room, and a Fomor stood guard outside.

Anya, the woman who had defied Cichal, peered out through a crack in the wall. Night had fallen and the stars were creating strange patterns across the sky. The shifting colours of the Northern Lights were clearly visible.

Something moved outside the hut and a solid shape suddenly blacked out the stars. The woman opened her mouth to scream, but the voice from the other side of the wall was unmistakably human.

'Ssssh. We're here to help you.'

'Who are you?' Anya whispered, peering out through the crack in the wooden wall.

'We're the people the Fomor are looking for. How many of the beasts are there?'

'Six, including the leader. They came on three nathair.'

On the other side of the wall, Paedur nodded, satisfied. He had counted six Fomor, including the one with the eye-patch, but he wanted to be sure.

The four humans and the Torc Allta had given the village a wide circle, and approached it from the northern side. Paedur had guessed that the Fomor would be watching the southern side of the village, expecting them to come that way.

They had slid down into the pit that encircled the village and then Ragallach had lifted them up and over the pointed fence, before hauling himself up and over. As he touched the soft earth, the sun sank down below the horizon in a blaze of pink and orange light and the were-beast assumed his boar shape. The transformation was far swifter than his earlier transformation, the bones and muscles seeming to shrink and draw in on themselves. The man-boar's facial features shifted, becoming more brutish, making him once again into the small reddish-pink pig.

Paedur had led them directly towards the Council Room, knowing that it was the only place where all the villagers could be kept. The four humans had moved through the deserted village with ease. With the exception of the single Fomor guarding the door of the Council Room, the remaining five beasts were scanning the southern horizon. The nathair were tied down to stakes in the centre of the village. Heavy leather hoods covered their heads, and they seemed to be sleeping.

There was just enough of a gap beneath the Council Room for Faolan, Ken and Ally to slide under, wrinkling their noses at the stench beneath the building. Ally was glad she couldn't see what she was lying in. Ragallach trotted in and lay down beside her, his head on her shoulder.

Paedur meanwhile had been peering through a crack in the logs when he'd been spotted by Anya. 'Is there any other way in?' he asked finally.

'There's only the one door,' she replied.

The bard nodded, and then, realising the woman probably couldn't see him, said, 'I'll see if I can cut my way in through the roof.' He climbed up the side of the building using the point of his hook to bite into the wooden logs. The roof was made of long, thick slices of turf laid down on a wooden frame. His razor-sharp hook sliced easily through the damp turf and into the framework beneath. He could hear pieces of turf dropping down onto the floor below.

When the tall, thin figure with the glittering hook dropped down lightly into the centre of the Council Room, there was a moment of shocked silence. The villagers had been expecting a warrior — they found they were looking at a young man, while Paedur was equally surprised to find himself surrounded by women. Pressing a finger to his lips for silence, he crossed the floor and, digging the point of his hook into a floorboard, eased it upwards. He pulled up a second and a third creating a large hole in the floor. The women crowded around, watching as the young bard reached down and lifted up a hairy pink pig. A red-haired young woman came up next, followed by someone who could only be her brother and finally a golden-haired young man.

Anya stepped forward. 'The Fomor are after *you*?' she asked, unable to hide the astonishment in her voice.

Paedur jerked his thumb at Faolan. 'The Fomor are after him. We just got mixed up in it by accident,' he added, looking around. He guessed there were about sixty women and children in the long room. There were all wearing the long heavy hooded fur and leather robes that were typical of the northern tribes. The leather was treated to keep off the rain and the fur kept them warm. Each outfit was painted in swirling, curling symbols, and no two outfits were the same. Paedur knew that every year the men and older boys of these isolated villages travelled into the Northlands hunting the huge snowcats and snowbears, which they would haul back to the villages on wooden sleighs. The carcasses would provide food and furs for the coming Cold Months.

'How can you defeat the Fomor?' Anya asked, looking directly at the bard. The women around her murmured and heads nodded in agreement.

Paedur attempted a brave smile. He finally shrugged. 'I don't know — yet!'

'The Fomor threatened to burn our homes,' Anya said quietly, watching the young bard. 'If they do that, it would be better for all of us if they killed us now.'

'Why?' Ken whispered.

'Because if we not do have have shelter when the Cold Months sweep in from the north, then we will die anyway. The winds that howl out of the Northlands can strip the flesh from humans, chill the blood in their veins, freeze their eyeballs to solid ice.' She paused and then added, 'And you have brought these creatures upon us.'

Paedur raised a hand, silencing the woman. 'I know that. We did not bring them here deliberately. Now, let us think...'

'They are invulnerable,' Faolan said quietly.

The bard shook his head. 'No-one is invulnerable. They are beasts, overgrown serpents. We can defeat them.'

Ken turned to the bard. 'These Fomor are serpent-folk?' he asked.

Paedur nodded. 'Their god is Quetaz, the Feathered Serpent.'

'In my time, reptiles like snakes hibernate...em,' he paused, seeing the look of confusion on the bard's face. 'That is, they go to sleep if it gets very cold.'

'I've never heard of that,' Paedur murmured, 'but I admit, I've never heard of the Fomor venturing into the Northlands.'

'It doesn't help us much,' Ally said quietly, her arms wrapped tightly around her body. Her teeth were chattering.

'It does. It does,' Ken was excited now. 'Can't you see? That's why they never travel into the Northlands. The cold slows them down, sends them to sleep.'

Paedur started to shake his head. 'I'm not sure...'

'Believe me,' Ken said earnestly. He turned to Faolan. 'Do you know any of the Windlore, do you know enough to call up an icy wind?'

Faolan touched the Book of the Wind in his pouch and shook his head. 'The Windlore is passed down through my family from father to son, mother to daughter. I've looked at the book, tried to memorise the first pages, but I don't understand it yet.' He shook his head again. 'I can't help you.'

'We could mount a surprise attack on the creatures,' a wild-haired young woman suggested. Anya looked doubtful.

Faolan tugged the bard's sleeve, drawing him to one side. He lifted the small leather-bound book from his pouch. 'You can read the Old Tongue, you know a little magic, could you not do something with this?'

Paedur shook his head. He touched the book with the flat of his hook — and a single blue spark snapped from the metal to the leather. 'These magical books — they're called grimores — are usually protected by a spell. Only very powerful magicians or members of a particular family can handle them safely.' He squeezed Faolan's shoulder. 'I think you will have to learn the Windlore soon.'

'I was thinking the same thing. If I knew a little now, it could save our lives.'

'You know a little magic,' Ken said to the bard. 'Could you not call up an icy wind or a snow storm?'

'Will it work?' Paedur asked.

'It will work,' Ken said firmly. 'I'd stake my life on it.'

'You are,' the bard said grimly. He sank down onto a straw mat on the wooden floor. Something Ken said had stirred a memory. Paedur had spent nearly eight years at Baddalaur, studying to be a bard. Becoming a bard was a long and difficult process: not only were the students expected to possess an exceptional memory, they were also trained in history, geography, weapons-craft, needlecraft, cookery, animal and herbal lore. A bard was expected to be able to survive on the road as he wandered from village to village, telling his stories, collecting his tales. Every three years, bards were required to return to Baddalaur to record the stories they had learned on their travels, and then these tales, in turn, were used to educate other bards. It was said that all a bard had to do was to hear or read a tale once and he would remember it forever, but very few bards were that good. Paedur was amongst the best.

Sitting in the centre of the floor of the Council Room, he closed his eyes and steadied his breathing. He was desperately trying to remember a story he had read several years ago. He recalled that it had come from the islands to the far south of the De Danann Isle. There had been a demon in the tale...a fire demon, who had lived deep in the core of a hollow mountain. Every evening the demon would burst up out of his mountain and rage through the villages on the islands, burning them to the ground, destroying crops and cattle with his fiery breath, turning the very stones to liquid.

A northern bard had been visiting the island then. Paedur frowned, desperately attempting to remember his name...Vanir, that was it, Vanir.

Vanir had climbed the mountain and chanted an ancient spell he had learned from his father. The spell had called down snow and ice on the hollow mountain, freezing it solid. The demon had come raging forth, but the snow had doused its flames.

And the words of that spell had been recorded with the story! Now all he had to do was to remember the words exactly. If he got even a single word wrong, it would mean disaster, because the icy spell would be drawn in on top of himself, freezing him solid.

The young bard raised his hook, light glittering from the half circle, and the crowded room fell silent. When he spoke his voice was a hoarse, croaking rasp, the words sharp and brittle — like ice.

*

Nres leaned on his spear, his huge yellow eyes blinking slowly. He scratched at a piece of flaking skin on the back of his arm. He'd be Shedding soon. Every season, the Fomor shed their skin, sliding out of the paper-thin covering to reveal a perfect new skin, with gleaming rainbow-hued scales. Most bondings — the human-kind called them weddings — were arranged about then, when the Fomor looked their best.

Right now, Nres didn't look his best. He was cold and tired and hungry. The ride northwards on the nathair had been uncomfortable and, although he would never admit it to anyone, Nres hated flying.

He stamped his clawed feet and curled his tail around his toes to keep them warm. He was cold. He thought briefly about the warm room full of the human-kind behind him. These females had been fierce fighters, better than many of the males he'd come up against in the past. He wondered if he should step inside — just to check them out, just to make sure everything was all right

— and to warm himself.

The Fomor yawned hugely, his enormous jaws opening wide, his breath smoking whitely on the air. He found he was looking up at the heavens, where the stars were glittering brilliantly. There were pictures in the stars, he knew, and even his own race, whose mythology was not as developed as the human-kind, told tales of the stars and the gods who lived in them.

That one there...that was the Home Star, sometimes called the North Star or the Guide Star...

As he watched the star blinked out.

And here was the Great Serpent, and the Little Serpent curling behind it...

They too disappeared.

Here was the Spear and the Sword, the Shield, and the Dagger...

One by one the stars vanished.

Straining, Nres could just about make out the cloud boiling across the sky, racing in from the north.

Something touched the Fomor's face, like a cold kiss. The creature hissed in alarm. There was another feather-soft touch on his face, and then his eyes, his forehead, his claws.

And it was cold, so cold...so cold.

Nres had never felt so cold before, never felt so sleepy.

He could hear shouting in the distance. It might have been Cichal, but the sound was so far away. The spear dropped from his numb claws, and he fell forward onto his knees. There was something on the ground. Something soft and white and cold.

He was so sleepy...so tired...so cold.

So very cold...so...

*

It snowed for no more than a thousand heartbeats, which was exactly how long it took for Paedur to chant the ancient snow-spell and then fall into an exhausted sleep.

*

Ally peered through the wooden door and saw that the entire village was covered in a thick coating of snow.

When they eventually ventured outside, they found the Fomor guard lying curled up on the ground. He was still alive, but had fallen into a deep, deep sleep.

They found four more of the Fomor were lying asleep close to the entrance to the village.

But there was no sign of Cichal.

The four humans set out early the following morning after breakfast. They left the village just before sunrise because they didn't want the villagers to see the pink pig turn into Ragallach the Torc Allta.

The snow which the bard had called up the night before still covered the ground, but the five Fomor were gone. Still sleeping, they had been dragged to their nathair and tied onto their bony backs. When the sun rose the nathair's hoods would be removed, and the creatures would take to the air, carrying the serpent-folk away with them. Only the gods knew where they'd end up.

There was no sign of Cichal. Faolan had speculated that the huge serpent had run at the first sign of snow, perhaps recognising it for what it was, and knowing the danger.

But that meant that he was still out there. Watching. Waiting.

Ally and Ken had been fitted out with clothing by the villagers: leather, long-sleeved jerkins with a high collar and smooth leather trousers, both of which were fur-lined. A long fur-lined cloak with a deep hood went over this, and knee-high fur-lined leather boots completed their wardrobe. Paedur was already wearing similar clothing — leather jerkin, leather trousers, worn leather boots. He had refused the offer of clothing, though Faolan had replaced his light summer garments with the heavier clothes. They had each been given gifts of water flasks and pouches containing curling strips of what looked like wood. Anya had informed them that it was dried meat. To make it soft and edible, strips were cut off and then chewed or boiled in water.

Ken, looking at the meat — it reminded him of a leather belt — decided he'd go hungry first.

Paedur had spent a few minutes talking with Anya, the Head-woman, discussing the location of the villages close to the Top of the World. Although these northern villages were isolated, they knew their nearest neighbours in every direction: they had to.

When he returned to the other three, who were standing by the gate with the pink pig running around their feet, his dark eyes were glittering. 'I think I've located your uncle, Faolan.'

'How long will it take us to get there?'

Paedur shrugged. 'Depends on what the weather is like. If we don't meet with any delays, we might reach there tonight, possibly early tomorrow.' He paused and added, 'And it would be better if we reached there tonight. We might not survive a night in the open.'

Ken nodded towards the horizon, which was already glowing pink with dawn. 'We had better get out of here, before our little friend here frightens the villagers.'

Waving their goodbyes, the four humans trekked off into the north. When they had dipped below the horizon, a shadowy figure slipped out of the gates and darted after them.

*

A hundred paces away, deep in the midst of a stunted thorn bush, Cichal watched them go with smouldering eyes. His long nails rammed into the hard earth and ripped out a large stone. Without any effort, he crushed it to dust.

*

They stopped for something to eat around noon.

Ragallach, now a Torc Allta again, had gone fishing in a narrow stream they had crossed. Standing statue-like in the middle of the icy fast-flowing stream, he had scooped out half a dozen fish in his hooves.

Faolan had cleaned the fish and cooked them on skewers over a low fire he had built in a circle of rocks. Ken and Ally had watched with a mixture of fascination and horror. Their eyes had grown rounder as they realised that he was going to cook the fish whole, with the head and tail...and then they realised that he expected them to eat the fish straight from the fire. Where they came from, fish came in long narrow rectangles covered in breadcrumbs. It was only when they reluctantly tried some that they realised that the fish they had been eating in their own time tasted nothing like freshly cooked fish! The three humans huddled around the fire carefully picking the fish from the bones, trying to ignore the noise of Ragallach crunching through a dozen raw fish.

Paedur sat a little apart from the others, with his back against a tall stone, his long legs stretched straight out in front of him. He didn't want any of the fish, preferring instead the little fruits and nuts the villagers had given them. They had made good time since they left the village and there was a chance they would reach one of the isolated villages in the region known as the Top of the World before nightfall. If Faolan's uncle wasn't in it, he hoped they'd be able to stay the night there before moving on: he didn't want to be out in this lonely land at night. The gods only knew what manner of strange beasts roamed it then. He smiled broadly when Ragallach squatted down in front of him.

The enormous boar's head tilted slightly, looking puzzled. 'When you human-kind twist your mouths like that, it is a sign of humour. What is so amusing?' Ragallach grunted.

'I was just wondering what manner of strange beasts walked this land at night — and you appeared. The coincidence is amusing.'

The Torc Allta snuffled and snorted, which was his laugh. 'The human-kind look just as strange to me, as I do to them.'

'I know that,' Paedur said gently.

'I often wonder how you human-kind survive,' the Torc Allta said softly, glancing at Faolan, Ally and Ken. 'Your skins are sensitive to heat and cold, you need to cook your food, you are neither swift, nor strong. How do you survive?'

Paedur tapped his forehead. 'We think...' He lifted his right hand and spread the fingers. 'And we can turn our thoughts into deeds with these.'

The Torc Allta nodded, although Paedur wasn't sure if the beast was actually agreeing with him.

Ragallach tilted his large head skywards. 'There is a storm coming,' he grunted.

Paedur nodded. 'I know...but how do you know?' he asked, curious.

The Torc Allta's pig-like snout wrinkled. 'I can smell it on the air. We will need to find shelter.'

'You are right,' Paedur said, standing up. Using his hook, he scrambled up onto the stone he'd been leaning against and looked northwards. Ragallach straightened; his head was on a level with the bard's waist.

The landscape ahead of them was flat and bleak as far as the horizon. The broken ground was cut and scoured as if a giant had slashed at it with a knife. There were no obvious signs of caves, nothing that would provide any shelter, and the few bushes that hugged the ground were stunted, twisted by the bitter wind.

'If we're caught out there in a storm, we're in real trouble,' Paedur murmured.

Ragallach tilted his head back, his snout wrinkling. Finally he shook his head. 'I can smell nothing but the wind and the rain. There are no human smells on the air.'

'Which means... ?' the bard asked.

'Which means we're a long way from any human settlement.'

'How close is the storm?'

'Close. But it might pass us by. Here in the Northlands, storms tend to be very localised — except during the Cold Months, when all of the Northlands is one huge storm.'

'We should go...just in case!'

Paedur had no doubt that both he and the Torc Allta would survive, but what about his companions? He slid down off the rock; all he could do would be to talk to them, tell them exactly what was happening, and allow them to make their own decisions. He knew he could force them to follow his lead: he knew he possessed the power to *make* them follow him. But he couldn't do that. They were about to make a life or death decision.

Ken knew that something was wrong. He had seen the look on the bard's face as he slid off the rock. Wiping his greasy fingers on his cloak and rubbing his sleeve across his mouth, he came slowly to his feet. He had come to rely on the bard: he seemed to know everything, he was so calm, so much in control. Ken knew that if Paedur was worried, then something serious must be wrong.

Ken was the only one facing the bard, so only he saw the creature appear on the rock behind him. He had a fleeting glimpse of something long, sleek and snow-white with red eyes and two long fangs coming out of its upper jaw. Even as he opened his mouth to cry out, the creature leapt at the bard...

Ragallach's massive arms shot out, catching the creature in mid-air, roughly shoving it away from the bard. It twisted and curled in the air, landing neatly on its feet, and immediately turned to face the humans and the Torc Allta. Its growl was a deep rumble, sounding like distant thunder.

'It's a sabre-toothed tiger,' Ally whispered, seeing the creature clearly for the first time.

'Snowcat,' Faolan corrected her. He pulled a burning stick from the fire, although he didn't think it would do much to frighten the creature.

It was enormous. Its massive head was on a level with the bard's chest, and the two long teeth that came down from its upper jaw were as long as his hand. Coal-black eyes regarded the humans hungrily.

'Little's known about them,' he muttered. 'They inhabit the cold northern icefields beyond Thusal and legend has it that they had once been big enough for a human to ride upon.'

'Do they eat humans?' Ken asked.

'They have a particular fondness for humans.'

Paedur backed away from the snowcat. He was desperately trying to recall what he knew about the creatures. The only piece of information he could remember however, was that they hunted in packs...

Even as the thought crossed his mind, two more of the

snow-white creatures appeared like ghosts on the rocks above them. He heard Ally scream and, although he didn't turn around, he guessed that another snowcat had appeared. They couldn't run, the snowcats would bring them down, and they couldn't fight four of the deadly creatures.

The enormous snowcats closed in, herding the humans around the remains of their fire. Ragallach kept turning to face the largest of the creatures. When the attack came, he knew that this one would lead it. The snowcats began to circle around the small group, their padded claws making no sound on the hard earth.

Faolan, Ally and Ken all held burning branches now, but the giant cats didn't even look at them.

Ragallach's massive paw fell on the bard's shoulder. 'If you have magic, use it now.'

'I can think of nothing...' Paedur began, and then he stopped. The largest cat was swaying from side to side and, as he watched, its piercing coal-black eyes rolled back in its head and it crashed over on its side.

A fleeting movement caught the Torc Allta's attention and he turned quickly. He had caught a glimpse of a figure in amongst the rocks. It was holding what looked like a long narrow tube. His sensitive hearing caught a hissing, spitting sound, and this time he actually *saw* the tiny needle-like dart appear on another of the snowcats' white fur. Like the first, the creature fell down without a sound. The remaining snowcats were confused. No longer concentrating on the humans they padded over to the fallen snowcats and nudged them with their muzzles.

'Let's go,' Paedur said urgently. 'Ally, go that way.' He nodded across the rocky plain. 'Ken, follow her; Faolan, you go next. Ragallach and I will take up the rear, just in case they decide to follow us. Walk, don't run.'

Throwing down the burning branch, Ally darted through a gap in the stones and ran out across the flat, grey stones. She immediately slowed to a brisk walk. The young woman was almost surprised that she no longer felt afraid. She'd been afraid when they'd first come into this strange land, she'd been frightened when they had seen the Fomor, and the nathair, and the damhan, the spider. She hadn't been quite so frightened when they'd encountered the Chopts, nor when the bard had demonstrated his magic, and she accepted Ragallach without question. It wasn't that she was unafraid. She had simply realised that it was an emotion she could control, and that maybe fear was an emotion which could become blunted.

Ken hurried up alongside his sister. There was a broad smile on his greasy face.

'What are you laughing about?' Ally demanded.

'I'm thinking that Mum or Dad should be here; think of the fun they'd have. And I've worked out something else. This island, this De Danann Isle, is probably the island which became known as Atlantis!'

'That's very interesting,' Ally said through gritted teeth. 'Tell me another time.'

'Sure. Atlantis was supposed to be a magical island which existed somewhere out in the Atlantic off the coast of Europe. Well, where does this magical island exist? Maybe the Skelligs were once part of Atlantis,' he continued.

'Look Ken, we'll talk about it later. Much later. When we're not being pursued by sabre-toothed tigers.'

'I think I'll write a book about all this,' Ken said, almost to himself. He smiled broadly at his sister's disgusted look.

'You can slow down now,' Faolan panted, coming up behind them. He stopped and looked back to where Paedur and Ragallach were walking slowly towards them. There was a slim fur-clad human walking alongside the bard.

'Who's that with them?' Ally wondered.

Faolan shook his head. 'Maybe the person who helped us back there,' he suggested. There was a sudden flash of white behind Ragallach as yet another snowcat appeared. It moved swiftly across the hard earth, padding silently on its huge paws. Ally and Faolan screamed their warnings at the same time.

The stranger beside Paedur dropped to one knee and a slender tube appeared in its hands. It raised the tube to its face and the snowcat suddenly tumbled over and slid along the stony ground, stopping almost at Ragallach's feet.

Ken and Ally followed Faolan back to where the bard, Ragallach and the stranger were bending over the still figure of the huge cat. They were in time to see the stranger push back the heavy hood and shake loose a head of chestnut-coloured curling hair.

'This is Megan,' Paedur said, without looking up. 'She's the daughter of Anya, the Headwoman of the village we stayed in last night. Megan decided she wanted some adventure, so she ran away to join us.'

'Lucky for us she did,' Ragallach grunted.

Ally crouched down beside the fur-clad girl. She was roughly her own age, she guessed, with a small heart-shaped face, and large, deep brown eyes almost the same shade as her hair. A thin leather band kept her hair back off her eyes. Her clothing matched that which the villagers had given the companions, the only difference being the small metal plates which had been sewn onto her jerkin.

'How did you stop the cats?' Ally asked.

The girl lifted what looked like a length of bamboo in her right hand. She held out her left hand and opened it. There was a brightly coloured needle of wood sitting in the palm of her hand.

'The darts are coated with a sleeping honey,' Megan said, her voice low and husky. 'The snowcats will sleep for half a day and awaken in a very bad humour.'

'Thank goodness you decided to follow us,' Ally smiled.

'As soon as I saw you, I knew my road lay with yours,' the young woman said shyly. She had a curiously precise way of speaking, as if every sentence had been carefully thought out in advance. 'Don't try to send me away,' she added evenly, looking from the red-headed girl to Paedur.

The bard ran his hand down the soft flesh of the cat for a final time before straightening. 'Faolan started out on this road on his own. I joined him and Ken and Ally joined us. Ragallach came next, and now you, Megan. I don't think I could send you away even if I wanted to. I see the hands of the gods in this; they obviously have something special in store for us.'

'It is an honour to be the chosen of the gods,' Ragallach

grunted.

Faolan patted his hairy arm. 'Those chosen by the gods usually don't live long enough to enjoy it,' he said with a smile.

'We should press on,' Paedur said urgently. 'There's a storm moving this way, and we don't want to get caught out in it. We haven't made it this far north just to die in a snow storm.'

For a single moment, when he had see the huge snowcats surrounding the human-kind, he had been tempted to help — but only because he feared that the Book of the Wind might be damaged if the snowcat ate Faolan!

Cichal had been following the figure who had set out after the human-kind when they left the village. The human stayed well back from the group, keeping to the cover of stones and stunted bushes, the brown furs it wore helping it to blend in with the dreary landscape. The human was so intent on following Faolan and his companions that he or she never once thought to look behind. If they had they would surely have spotted the Fomor.

Cichal was determined to track the human-kind to their destination. The boy had been given the Book of the Wind for a reason, possibly to pass it on to someone or to hide it away in some secret place. Even though he knew the dangers of travelling into the cold Northlands, Cichal pressed on. He had already lost face with the Emperor, and the Emperor did not forgive mistakes easily. The long hall that led to the Emperor's Council Chamber was lined with incredibly life-like statues. The statues were perfect in every detail...except that the expression on every subject's face was always one of terror and horror. They had once been living beings, but they had angered or upset or annoyed the Emperor in some way...and been turned to stone by his magic.

Balor the Emperor ruled the De Danann Isle by fear. He was

part-Fomor, part-human, and he possessed the great strength of his father, who had been a Fomor warrior, and the cunning and magic of his mother, who had been a powerful sorceress. He was a giant of a man, and looked human, except for the metal mask that covered half his face. No-one had ever seen what lay under the mask, and lived. Those who saw what lay beneath the shining metal were instantly turned to stone. Throughout the De Danann Isle, the Emperor was known as Balor of the Evil Eye.

And Cichal had no desire to see what lay beneath the metal half-mask. He had to bring the book or the boy, or both, back to the Emperor.

Shortly after sunrise he had been surprised to find that there was another person with the human-kind. At first he had thought it was an adult, but when the figure turned, Cichal realised he was looking at a Torc Allta, one of the Were-Beasts. He remembered then the small pink pig that had accompanied the humans. This was an added complication. The Fomor had considered attacking Faolan and his companions himself: after all, what could four human whelps do against a Fomor Officer? But the Torc Allta, although he didn't look fully grown, was powerful and dangerous. So, if Cichal was going to attack the human-kind, he would have to do it at night, when the Torc Allta was in its boar shape, and the humans were tired. But at night, it was so cold that he could barely move. All he wanted to do was sleep. He also knew that if they went much further north, he wouldn't be able to follow them.

Cichal had watched the small human save them from the snowcats. The Fomor had been hiding in the rocks, quite close to the fur-clad figure, and he had seen how powerful the blow-pipe was. This was another danger. A poison that could knock out the snowcats could easily knock out a Fomor.

The small figure turned out to be a young female, and the five humans and the Torc Allta had walked away from the fallen snowcats together.

Cichal hissed in frustration. He had set out to find one human, now he was up against five and a were-beast. Maybe he was getting too old for all this. Perhaps it was time to think about returning to the Fomor Isles and growing grapes. The Fomor made the finest wines in the De Danann Isles. If he had followed his mother's advice, he'd be there now, sitting in the sun, watching the grapes darken, instead of freezing in this dreary land with the threat of being permanently frozen, either by the weather or Balor, hanging over his head.

The Fomor paused by the fallen snowcats. He was surprised to find that they were still alive; the darts hadn't poisoned them as he had thought, merely sent them to sleep. His single eye spotted the tiny darts in the white fur and he delicately plucked one out, his forked tongue darting out, tasting the air around it, identifying the mixture by the scents. It had a sweet honey-like smell, along with something sharp and bitter, probably some sleeping herb. He slipped the dart into his pouch; maybe Balor's physicians might be able to find some use for it in their medicines. He thought briefly about making a meal off one of the snowcats, but Faolan and his companions were already disappearing into the distance. With a sigh, Cichal settled his sword on his back and took off after them. He should have listened to his mother, he decided.

The company continued to move northwards throughout the day. Twice more they were threatened by snowcats, but the small human's darts put them to sleep, and the group didn't even slow down. Cichal got a fright when he was passing one of the sleeping creatures. The dart that had stuck in it must have fallen out or just grazed it, making it dozy. As the huge Fomor passed it, the creature rose up and growled at him. Cichal glared at the snowcat and opened his massive jaws, showing the triple row of triangular teeth. The snowcat dropped its tail between its legs and staggered off into the rocks.

Snow began to fall as the sun dipped below the horizon.

The flakes were tiny, drifting down from an almost cloudless sky, but Cichal feared them as much as if they had been enemy spears. If the cold overcame him now, it wouldn't kill him, but it would probably put him to sleep until the Warm Months. However, there were a lot of hungry animals between now and the Warm Months, and while some of them might find the Fomor scales just a little too tough to chew on, he didn't particularly want them trying.

The huge Fomor stopped in the middle of the stony track he was following. He had a choice: either he continued on after the humans or he sought shelter. His every instinct warned him to look for some place to spend the night at least, some place he could build a fire and keep warm, but Cichal was a Fomor Officer, and he wasn't going to give up now.

Another flurry of snow made him change his mind.

Leaving the track, he climbed a low rocky hill, looking for a cave or a crevice he could hide out in. At the top of the hill, he found he was looking out over a narrow inland lake. There was an island in the centre of the lake. In the centre of the island, surrounded by a tall wall of pointed tree trunks, was a small village. A narrow floating bridge ran from the shore to the island...and the five humans were walking boldly across the bridge. They had reached the mid-point when the wooden door in the fence was drawn back and a tall, yellow-haired man strode out. Even from a distance, and despite the fading light, Cichal could see the resemblance to Faolan. This was why the boy had travelled northwards. There was another Windlord!

They spoke together for a few moments and then turned towards the village. The gates were closing behind them when the red-haired human female appeared. She seemed to be looking for something. A small pink pig appeared on this side of the lake and darted out across the bridge. The female scooped it up into her arms and darted through the gates. The gate slammed shut behind her. In the still air, Cichal heard what sounded like a wheel turning. Two ropes appeared up out of the water. They were connected to the middle of the bridge and went back into two holes on either side of the gate. With barely a ripple, the floating bridge split in two and rose up out of the water. When it was pointing straight up into the air, providing additional protection for the gate, which was the weakest spot in the wall, two villagers appeared on the wall behind it and tied it securely to the logs.

Now this was something Cichal could understand. The village

seemed to be strongly defended. Without the bridge in place, an attacker would have to cross the lake by boat and even then the wall would have to be climbed.

However, it also meant that the villagers couldn't get out — and the village was still vulnerable to attack from the air. So it should be possible to drop in Fomor Troops from nathair. They could lower the bridge and the rest of the Troop could come across. If it was done properly, they could take the village without any fighting.

Cichal slid back down the slope. He discovered a shallow cave hidden beneath an overhanging slab of rock and crawled into it. Once inside he scooped up the rough stone, shale and grey sand that covered the floor and used it to block up the entrance. When he was finished, the entrance to the cave was invisible from outside and there was a deep hollow in the cave where he could curl up quite comfortably. Although it was almost pitch black in the small cave, Cichal had no trouble seeing. It reminded him a little of the room where he had hatched. In his home on the Fomor Isles, his mother still kept the remains of the shell he'd hatched from.

Sitting cross-legged in the deep hollow he'd made, he spread his cloak out on the ground in front of him. He slid his knife from its sheath and placed it on the cloak. He then lifted a small stone bottle from his belt pouch and placed it alongside the knife. The smoothly polished wooden cup that went everywhere with him followed.

Cichal paused before continuing. He'd never tried this before, although the Emperor's magicians who'd created the simple spell had demonstrated it often enough.

First he poured the contents of the stone jar into the wooden cup. It was like liquid silver and gave off a faint silvery light. When he leaned over the cup, his own distorted reflection looked back up at him. Picking up the knife, he cut off the topmost button of his tunic. Each uniform button usually bore the likeness of Balor, but this one was blank. Keeping his eyes and mouth tightly closed, Cichal dropped the button into the silvery liquid.

Even with his eyes closed he could see and feel the sudden

flash of light and heat. A stench of rotten eggs tickled his nostrils. When he'd counted to twenty as he'd been taught, he opened his eyes and looked into the bowl.

Instead of his own reflection looking back at him, a scowling human face looked up from the bowl. Or rather, half a human face: the left side was completely covered in a shining metal mask. He was looking at Balor!

Knowing that he had less than twenty heartbeats to relay his news, Cichal blurted, 'Greetings Lord Balor, Emperor of the De Danann Isle. I have tracked the human whelp to a village at the Top of the World, beyond the Ice-Fields of Thusal. The village is situated on an island in the middle of a lake. Send me a Troop of Fomor and nathair. I will not fail you.'

'I will send a hundred Fomor on fifty nathair.' Balor's voice was thin and distant, like the faintly heard buzzing of a fly. 'Make an example of these people. Destroy the village. Burn it to the ground. Bring the boy back to me. Do not fail me,' he added, and although there was no anger, no emotion in his voice, the mighty Fomor Officer shivered with terror.

'Faolan!'

The man who came out to greet Faolan was so like him that the two could have been mistaken for father and son. The tall golden-haired, golden-bearded man swept the boy up in his arms, holding him without any effort. He looked slim, but he was obviously immensely strong, and the only indication of his age were the lines on his face and around his sky-blue eyes. His clothes had once been of the finest quality, but had now been patched and repatched so often that they resembled a quilt, with only a hint of the original uniform he'd once worn.

'You're in trouble,' he said simply, looking past Faolan to the group who accompanied him.

'We need to talk, uncle.'

'Of course. Follow me.' He put Faolan down on the ground and turned away, moving quickly through the dozens of small wooden cottages that crowded the island. His cottage was set a little apart from the others, nestling right up against the wall. The framework of wood had been covered with thick mud which had been allowed to harden until it was almost as solid as stone. There was grass growing out of the turf roof. It was dark inside the hut and smoke from the small fire in the middle of the floor curled around the room, making them all cough, and the small pig snuffle and snort.

While Faolan's uncle coaxed the fire to a low blaze, the

companions seated themselves around the wall facing him, allowing themselves to relax; their journey ended here.

'This is my uncle Lugh,' Faolan began, 'a Windlord, the last of the Windriders.'

Lugh's teeth flashed whitely in the gloom. 'It's been a long time since I rode the wind,' he said gently. 'But first, introductions and then we can talk. You first,' he said, looking at the bard who was sitting at his right.

'I am Paedur, training to be a bard at Baddalaur.'

Lugh bowed politely and looked at the red-haired girl.

'I am Alison...well, most people call me Ally. My brother and I were pulled back through time when Faolan's father used a magical spell.'

'My name is Kenneth, sir, and we're hoping you'll be able to send us back to our own time on the Timewinds.'

'I am Megan, warrior-maiden of the Bear Tribe. I joined this troop but lately.'

'And the pig is really a Torc Allta,' Faolan added. He was sitting on his uncle's left-hand side. 'In the daylight it takes its were-beast shape and during the hours of darkness it becomes a pig.'

Lugh looked more closely at the pink pig, which was nestling in Ally's arms. 'I thought it was more than just a pig,' he nodded. 'Now, tell me what happened. Faolan, you first.'

Taking a deep breath, Faolan launched into his story. He knew if he paused or hesitated the tears would come. So far he'd managed to avoid thinking too closely about what had happened to his parents and sister. The flight into the Northlands had helped, but this was first time he'd been forced to face it.

'Balor has my parents and sister,' he said simply. He took a deep breath and continued. 'The Emperor sent for us a while ago. He wanted to become the Master of all the Old High Magics, the Elemental Magics. He could control fire and water and make the earth move — all he needed was the Windlore to control the element of air. Father refused him and we fled that same day. Balor was furious. He sent Cichal the Fomor after us. He commands the Emperor's personal bodyguard, so you can see how desperately he wanted the Windlore. We fled across country, stopping at tiny villages, hiding, always hiding. We hoped to reach the coast and sail to the lands in the east. Father said he could call up a wind to push us along. But the Fomor caught up with us at Baddalaur, the College of Bards. There was a chase. Father held them off with some windmagic.' The boy smiled, remembering. 'He called up a storm in the middle of the library — we think that's when Ken and Ally were pulled back by the Timewinds.'

'That's possible,' Lugh muttered.

'But the effort of magic exhausted father and so mother gave me the book...' he pulled the small book from his pocket, 'and told me to bring it to you.' He held the book towards his uncle, but Lugh didn't take it. Faolan let his hand drop. 'I was chased by one of the Fomor; he was going to eat me, he said. He would have too, but Paedur saved me. We escaped by running down the steps on the outside of Baddalaur's walls. We met Ken and Ally there. The Fomor, led by Cichal himself, chased us, but we stole one of their nathair and flew northwards. We were attacked by Chopts, but Paedur saved us and later Ally rescued the pig from a trap. In the morning the pig transformed into a Torc Allta just in time to save us from another Chopt. We came across a village that had been taken over by the Fomor, but again, using Ken's plan and Paedur's magic, we managed to overpower the creatures and save the villagers. They supplied us with food and clothes. We set off just before dawn this morning, but we were attacked by snowcats. I don't know what would have happened if Megan hadn't come along and rescued us by knocking the cats out with her sleeping darts.' He shrugged his thin shoulders. 'And that's more or less it.'

Lugh glanced at Paedur and attempted a laugh. 'There's enough material here for a saga, eh?'

The bard nodded but said nothing. He kept staring intently at Lugh.

'Why have you come here?' Lugh asked Faolan finally.

The boy looked surprised. 'Because mother told me to give you this book.'

Lugh shook his head. 'I can't take the book.'

There was a shocked silence. 'But you must. You have to. You're a Windlord...'

'I'm not.'

Faolan nodded fiercely, suddenly close to tears. 'Yes you are. You're the finest Windlord in the De Danann Isles, the most famous Windrider.'

'That was a long time ago, Faolan,' Lugh said gently. 'Things change, people change.'

'But...'

'Let him speak,' Paedur said sharply, and Faolan immediately fell silent.

'I see you've already learned the Tone of Command,' Lugh commented. 'When I was at court, I once saw a bard command an entire army to lay down their arms — and they did so. Gerard, I think his name was...'

'Gahred,' Paedur said with a thin smile. 'He was my uncle.'

Lugh looked back at Faolan and then at the book he still held in his hand. 'The Book of the Wind, the Windlore,' he said almost sadly. 'I can clearly remember the first day I opened that book and began to read. I was so frightened.'

'Lugh, I need you to rescue my parents and sister. Cian is your own brother.'

'And we need you to send us back to our own time,' Ally said quickly.

'I wish I could help...'

'You have to help,' Ken said loudly.

'I cannot.'

'Tell us why,' Paedur said sharply. Lugh started to shake his head.

'We've come a long way to find you,' Paedur said quietly, 'you owe us an explanation.'

'I suppose I do,' Lugh sighed. He took a deep breath and then nodded. 'The years have turned twenty times since I first came to this village. That was just after the war with the Toltecs, the copper-skinned humans from the lands to the west. The war had been raging for four year-cycles, and was fought on land and sea and with magic. But their warriors were brave and fearless, and their magicians were just as powerful as ours, so neither side could gain the upper hand.

'Balor was Emperor then. He was a strong and powerful ruler then, not evil and cruel as he is now, and he decided that he wanted the war to end. He approached the four Lords of the Elements: the Master of Fire, the Lord of the Sea, the Earthlord and the Windlord, and asked us to use our powers to bring the war to an end.

'But the Lords of the Elements refused...theirs was the Old High Magic, it could not be used for ill, nor could it be commanded by any one man.

'Balor raged, but there was little he could do. He knew he was not powerful enough to go up against the four Lords himself.

'But one of the Lords was not in agreement with his brothers. He thought that the Old High Magic should be used to bring the war to a conclusion. He struck a deal with Balor and in a day and a night, used his powerful magic to drive the Toltecs back to their homeland, destroying their boats so that they could never put to sea again, smashing their homes, ravaging their fields so that they would go hungry. Who knows how many died in that day and night, but I'm sure it was small compared to the numbers who died in the days and seasons following the attack. Famine and disease swept across the Toltec land and a once mighty race was reduced to being little more than savages. It will take them hundreds of year-cycles to rebuild their once proud civilisation.

'Balor was delighted.

'The De Danann and Fomor army marched through the Toltec land and stripped it of much of its wealth, especially its gold, for which it was famous.

'The Lords of the Elements were furious of course. They cursed their brother who had abandoned them. They combined their magics to strip the Renegade Lord of all his magical powers; and they finally banished him...to a tiny village at the Top of the World.

'I was the Renegade Lord.'

No-one broke the long silence that followed.

Lugh sighed. 'I did what I thought was right. But I wasn't right. I alone am responsible for countless deaths. Because of me a proud civilisation fell.'

Faolan drew in his breath in a great ragged sigh. 'I never knew,' he whispered hoarsely.

'The Lords of the Elements were so ashamed of what I had done that they stripped my name from their history books and records.' He looked sharply at the bard, 'Surely you knew?'

Paedur shook his head. 'I know the story of course. I didn't know it was you. In the legends, the Renegade Lord left the World of Men in search of his magic.'

Lugh nodded. 'I left the World of Men, that is true, but I want nothing to do with magic.'

'Then our journey has been for nothing,' Faolan continued. 'You cannot help us, you cannot help my parents and sister.'

'And we're trapped here forever,' Ken said quietly.

'I'm sorry,' Lugh said simply, 'I have no power left. I wish I could help.'

'You can,' Paedur said with a thin smile. He stood up and walked around the room, finally stopping behind Faolan.

Lugh turned to look at him. 'I have no magic,' he said.

'Do you need magic to teach?'

The companions looked at the bard blankly. And then Ragallach, followed by Ally, began to smile as they realised what the bard was saying. Paedur dropped his hook onto Faolan's shoulder. 'Teach Faolan the Windlore. Make him the new Windlord!'

The cold awoke Ken. He sat up on the hard wooden boards and found that the thick sleeping furs had slid onto the reed-covered floor at the foot of the narrow bed. Swinging his feet out onto the icy floor, he pulled up the thick fur blanket and wrapped it around himself.

He had never felt so cold in his life. The bard had told him that one of the reasons the Chopts hadn't developed iron weapons or tools was because the metal became brittle and snapped in the intense cold. But what Ken found frightening was that the Cold Months — which he supposed meant winter — hadn't even arrived yet. This was their equivalent of autumn.

There was only one window in the hut. There was no glass in it, but what looked like a thin shell had been placed across the opening, allowing a pale watery sunlight to filter through during the day. At night it was covered over with a heavy fur to keep out the chill. Crossing to the window, Ken pulled back the curtain. A corner of the shell had been broken and the air coming through the small hole was bitter, making his eyes sting, burning its way into his lungs. His teeth began to ache.

A full moon was riding high in the sky. It looked larger than Ken remembered it from his own time, and he wondered if it was closer to the earth. The sky was so clear that he could easily pick out the features on the moon. Paedur had said that the moon had once been part of the earth, but the huge chunk of land had been torn from the ground and hurled up into the sky by a powerful magician on the other edge of the world.

Ken was about to turn away when a shape crossed the moon. Long and slender, with huge beating wings, it looked like a dragon. A second and a third followed. Ken was turning towards the door when it burst open and Paedur raced into the room.

'Fomor on nathair,' he shouted. 'Dozens of them. We're surrounded.'

There was pandemonium in the village. The inhabitants lined the walls, their weapons pitifully few against the might of the Fomor. The people were mostly fishers and hunters, with some craftsmen who worked in bone and wood. What happened in the lands to the south were no concern of theirs. They had nothing to do with the Emperor and his Fomor guards. But now a force of the Emperor's finest warriors on their flying serpents had descended on their village. The flat, white snowfields on the other side of the lake were dark with the hissing, rustling flying serpents and their Fomor riders.

'Why don't they attack?' Faolan asked, peering over the edge of the wall.

Lugh shook his head. He ran his hands through his golden hair, pulling it back off his face. 'I don't know. Maybe they don't like to fight at night, like the Chopts.'

'But it will be dawn soon. What will happen then?'

Lugh shook his head. 'I don't know.'

'They won't attack with the nathair,' Paedur said quietly, coming up behind them. They were standing on the little walkway that ran along the top of the wall. It was barely wide enough for two people to pass by, but it was now crowded with the villagers.

'Why won't they attack?' Faolan asked.

'For the same reason the Fomor have never explored the lands to the west or east of the De Danann Isle. The nathair will not — cannot — fly over water. It has something to do with the reflections thrown back by the water; it affects their balance. Maybe Cichal was hoping to take the nathair high into the air and bring them down directly on top of the village. But I'm afraid he will find the air too thin and too cold; the nathair won't fly in it. No, the nathair are useless. When the Fomor come at us, they'll have to come on land or by water.'

Lugh suddenly grinned. 'There is only one bridge and we control that, and coming by water might prove difficult. The Fomor won't want to cross that: they know it's below freezing in there. If they fall in, they'll freeze solid. Also, the waters are filled with sliver-eels.' He held up his little finger. 'No bigger than this, but with incredibly sharp teeth. They burrow deep into their victim, live there for a while and then eat their way out.'

'What are we going to do?' Faolan whispered. 'They can't get in, but we can't get out. They'll starve us out probably,' he added.

'How much food have we got?' Paedur asked Lugh.

'Enough. Remember, these people are used to being trapped on this island. During the last season, we were confined to our huts for twenty full days and nights while a storm raged outside. The lake water is fresh, and is drawn from a well in that small hut close to the centre of the village.'

Paedur nodded. He turned around to look out across the village. The situation wasn't entirely hopeless. The next move was the Fomor's. They would attack, and it would have to be soon; they couldn't afford to stay too long in this cold climate. The chill would slow them down, make them stupid and dull, encourage mistakes, maybe even send them to sleep...

Megan made her way along the crowded walkway towards the bard. Although her face was set in a grim smile, her deep brown eyes were sparkling. She was holding her bow and arrow in one hand and her blowpipe in the other.

'I came with you for adventure,' she said excitedly. 'I did not realise just how much adventure.'

'Maybe too much?' Paedur asked.

'One can never have too much adventure,' she said quickly.

'I don't think the villagers will agree with you,' the bard remarked. 'I'm not sure if I agree with you. We seem to be trapped here: I would say our case is pretty hopeless.'

The Warrior Maid shook her head quickly. 'No case is ever completely hopeless. We have your magic, we can use that. All the villagers I've spoken to can throw a spear and fire a bow — they have to, since their livelihood depends on it. They are a brave people and they're angry now because the Fomor have invaded their land.' She paused for a moment and added, 'I can make up my sleeping-honey from amongst the stores here. I'm not sure how effective it will be against the beasts, but we can try.' She looked up to where the sky was paling towards the dawn, steel-grey clouds massing on the horizon. 'There will be snow before this day is done. The Fomor fear snow. That will force them to attack.'

'Do it,' Paedur commanded Megan. 'Take whatever you need; make the sleeping-honey. And Megan,' he added, 'instruct the villagers how to defend themselves.' He watched the small dark girl drop lightly to the ground and then dart through the crowd. Not only would her advice be of practical use, it would also give the villagers something to think about. And while they were working on that, they weren't thinking about the enormous force of Fomor camped across the lake. 'If we had a Windlord we wouldn't have a problem,' he remarked quietly, looking from Lugh to Faolan. 'A Windlord would be able to conjure us up a wind that would scatter this army to the ends of the world.'

Lugh followed the direction of the bard's gaze and suddenly realised what he was saying. He shook his head quickly. 'You're not seriously suggesting...' he began. 'I mean, it took me nearly eight year-cycles to master the Windlore.'

'Faolan doesn't have to master all the Windlore,' Paedur snapped. 'That can come later. All he has to be able to do now is to call up and control the wind elementals, maybe to ride the wind back to Falias to rescue his parents and,' he nodded to the foot of the ladder where Ken and Ally waited, 'he needs to be able to send our friends here back to their own time.'

'It took me eight year-cycles,' Lugh repeated.

The bard looked at the gathered army. 'You have half a day, maybe a day at most,' he said without looking around.

'Impossible!'

'Nothing is impossible,' Paedur said simply. 'The Book of the Wind is magical, is it not?' He continued as Lugh nodded slowly.

'Magic can be taught...or it can be absorbed.'

Lugh shook his head quickly. 'That's too dangerous. The Windlore is too powerful, it has to be learned little by little.'

'We have no choice.'

Ally stood in the doorway of the small, dark hut where she'd spent the night. Despite her fur and leather clothing, she was still bitterly cold, and the fear, which she thought she'd lost, had returned. She was really frightened now.

She watched Megan organising the villagers. Ken was by her side, distributing weapons, while Ragallach, now in his Torc Allta form, was using his massive strength to build up a barrier before the gates. Ally had thought that the Torc Allta would have terrified the villagers, but she guessed that they were more frightened of the Fomor army than a single beast.

Paedur was standing on the narrow walkway, looking out over the lake at the Fomor. With the sun glinting off his hook and his cloak twisting and curling in the breeze, he looked like some ancient god. There was no sign of Faolan or Lugh.

Wrapping her cloak around her shoulders, Ally padded across the hard ground to where Megan and Ken were sorting through a pile of arrows. The Warrior Maid was instructing her brother how to pick only the best arrows.

'Can I help?' she asked.

Megan nodded. 'I was about to ask for your help. I need to prepare a batch of sleeping-honey. It is a delicate, dangerous task, and in my village, it is a recipe known only to women. We are forbidden to share it with men.' She glanced at Ken and he smiled broadly at the idea of being called a man. Megan slipped her arm through Ally's and led her away towards the storerooms.

*

By the time the sun had moved much higher in the sky, an unnatural calm had fallen over the village. Everyone was waiting for the Fomor attack.

From his position close to the gate, Paedur could see the massed Fomor troop. There were at least a hundred of the beasts, all of them heavily armed and wrapped up against the cold. Enormous fires had been built close to the shore and the beasts huddled around them, feeding the fires with small pots of a white sticky liquid: firestone sap, Paedur guessed. He had recognised Cichal by the sunlight flashing off his eyepatch, and although the beasts' expressions were almost unreadable to humans, Paedur could have sworn that the Fomor was smiling.

Paedur turned to look back over the walled island. With the exception of the old people and the young children, everyone was lining the walls or in position around the village. Ragallach stood guard outside the hut where Megan and Ally were preparing the sleeping-honey, and there were two guards on duty outside the hut where Lugh was teaching Faolan the Windlore. It was a desperate chance, Paedur knew, but it was all they had.

*

It was dark inside the hut, and although the fire had been allowed to die down, the air was still rich with the smell of turf and animal dung which had been used for fuel. The heat still lingered too, trapped within the thick wooden walls and the turf floor and roof. It was also completely silent.

And Faolan found the silence the most frightening of all.

Outside, he knew the villagers were preparing to defend themselves against the Emperor's finest warriors, the virtually invincible Fomor, and yet here he was sitting on a reed mat in the darkened hut with the Book of the Wind in his lap. For all he knew the battle could be raging right outside the door and he would still hear nothing. He knew his uncle Lugh was in the hut with him, but he had lost all sense of direction and didn't know exactly where.

'In the beginning was Danu and Dagda Ollathair, the All-Mother and All-Father.' Lugh's voice came from behind Faolan, making him jump. He turned towards the sound, but when his uncle spoke again, his voice was coming from directly in front of him. 'They had existed in the Void for an eternity before they created this world to amuse themselves. Danu gave water and air from the core of her own body, Dagda gave earth and fire from his, and from these elements they spun the web that created this world.

'And because these four Elements, earth and air, fire and water were once part of the gods, they too had an intelligence and life and possessed the powerful magic of the gods, the Old High Magic.

'The Elements in turn created other minor gods and godlings, and eventually created Man and Beast. How Man got control of the Elements is another tale, but when this world was very young, about the time when, it is said, there was but one continent covering the face of the earth, four brothers braved the Elements and discovered their secret. Each of the brothers dedicated himself to a particular magic: theirs was a terrible secret, an awesome power, because whosoever controls the Elements, controls the World.

'We are the Windlords, Faolan.

'For generations our family has possessed the secret of the Element of air. It is the most powerful of all the Elements. We can control the wind, bring storms or calm the raging hurricane. We can change the weather, even change the air in men's lungs. All these, and much more, are within a Windlord's grasp.

'But when people think of the Windlords, they think of a Windrider, a warrior riding a steed of air. I was once a Windrider, Faolan. Let us see if I can teach you a little of what I knew. Open the book.'

'It's dark, uncle,' Faolan protested.

'Open the book.'

Faolan opened the book.

*

Cichal the Fomor drew back his arm and hurled his spear at the wooden wall surrounding the village. The spear, which was taller than the Fomor, arced into the air. Long slits had been cut into the head of the spear, and the air streaming through these screamed and whistled harshly. The spear struck the wooden wall close to the young bard, the metal head actually bursting right through the wood.

The villagers murmured angrily, and several drew their bows back, ready to fire.

'Wait,' Paedur commanded. He crossed to where the spear had broken through the wall and then sliced through the wooden shaft with his hook. He held up the spear's metal head. There was a bright yellow ribbon tied around it. Paedur touched the ribbon with his fingertips. 'They want to talk.'

'It's a trap,' Ken said quickly, joining the bard. Although the boy had never used a bow in his life, he was carrying a bow and a quiver of arrows.

Paedur shook his head. 'Unlikely. The Fomor might be many things, but they have a rigid code of honour. However,' he added with a smile, 'I don't think we'll open the gates.' He looked down over the edge of the fence. There was a small circular wood and hide boat bobbing in the icy water. 'Ask Ragallach if he'll lower me down. I'll row over and see what they want.'

'But they'll kill you and eat you!' Ken protested.

'I am a bard,' Paedur said simply. 'We enjoy what's called the Emperor's Privilege: it means we can travel to the four ends of the De Danann Isle without hindrance. Anyway,' he added, 'bards don't taste too good.'

Ragallach was even less enthusiastic about the idea when he returned with Ken. 'Fomor are treacherous,' he grunted. 'They will keep you, trade you for Faolan.'

Paedur smiled. 'That's simple then. Don't swap.'

'Simpler if you didn't go,' the Torc Allta said. 'Fomor like

134

human meat,' he added.

'But it buys us time,' Paedur said slowly. 'Time for Megan to prepare her sleeping-honey, time to Faolan to learn a little of the Windlore.'

The Torc Allta shook his great head. 'This is foolish. All we have to do is to remain here. We can hold off a Fomor attack and let the weather do the rest for us.'

The young bard shook his head. 'They're well wrapped against the weather and those fires will help them remain awake.' He nodded to where the spear had broken through the wall. 'We wouldn't be able to hold them off for ever. No,' he shook his head again. 'I'll go over and talk to them. Lower me down on a rope.'

'I'll find a rope,' Ken said quietly.

Paedur waited until Ken had dropped to the ground and then he turned to Ragallach. They had struck up a curious friendship in the past two days. In many ways they were very similar: they were both loners, and were both happy and content in their own company. Ragallach's size and features and the bard's hook hand set them apart, made them objects of curiosity. 'If anything happens to me over there,' he said very quietly, not looking at Ragallach, 'I want you to take Faolan and Lugh, Ally and Ken and lead them to safety. Megan can look after herself. If she'll go with you then so much the better. Faolan must complete his training as a Windlord. Only he can rescue his parents and sister, only he can send the two strangers back to their own time.'

'Where will I go, where will I take them?' the big were-beast asked.

'Head to the east. Take to the sea. There are lands to the east, fresh green islands, uninhabited, unexplored. There is a primitive civilisation clustered around a huge inland sea. You should be safe there.'

Ken returned with a thin rope that was made from twisted and woven reeds. 'I'm not sure how strong it is,' he said, tugging at it.

'Stronger than you think,' Ragallach grunted, tying it around the bard's waist. He looked at the enormous bundle of rope and then measured the distance to the land. 'Don't untie the rope,' he said slowly, knowing that the human-kind sometimes found his snuffling snorting speech difficult to understand. 'When you reach the shore opposite, don't untie the rope. If you are in trouble, raise your left hand.' He lifted the thin cord. 'I will try to pull you back.'

Paedur was about to shake his head, but nodded instead. 'It's worth a try.'

Ken, who was looking towards the shore, asked, 'How do we let our friends there know we're going to talk to them?'

'Give Ragallach your bow,' Paedur commanded.

Ken passed across the weapon and a single arrow. In the Torc Allta's huge paws it looked like a toy. The bard untied the yellow ribbon from the spear head and tied it tightly around the arrow head.

Without saying a word, the Torc Allta drew back the weapon until it threatened to snap and then released the arrow. It hissed through the air to land on the hard ground between Cichal's feet.

The Fomor looked down at the length of wood quivering close to his long-nailed claws and then he stamped on the arrow, snapping it in half, driving it deep into the earth.

'I think you've annoyed it,' Ken smiled.

The bard was about to climb up onto the rampart when Megan and Ally appeared. Paedur waited until they climbed up the wooden ladder to stand on the ramparts. They were both streaked with soot and smelt of herbs and spices, their eyes were red-rimmed and their fingers were stained green from their preparations. Megan handed Paedur a small stone jar.

'Sleeping-honey in powder form,' she said simply. 'Blow it in the face of your adversary and he will fall asleep. I've trebled the dosage so it should work on a Fomor...but I don't really know.'

Paedur slipped the small jar into his belt pouch. 'Excellent. Thank you.' He stopped suddenly and looked at Megan. 'How much of this have you made?'

'Not much. I've made some in powder form, but the rest is in a paste which can be coated onto spears and arrows.'

'Make more powder,' the bard suggested. He looked at Ragallach and nodded. Without a word the Torc Allta lifted up the rope and lowered the bard out over the edge.

'What's he doing?' Ally demanded loudly.

'Buying us time,' Ragallach said simply. He glanced back over his shoulder to the hut where Faolan and Lugh were working. 'Let's hope Faolan doesn't let him down.'

The light was blinding.

It seemed to lift off the pages and pour out of the book in a solid sheet of light that was almost painful to look at. Faolan's instinct was to squeeze his eyes shut, but he could hear his uncle's commanding voice, ordering him to, 'Look at the book...look at the book...look at it...look...look...look.'

With an enormous effort of will, Faolan looked at the book. The letters seemed to dance on the page, shimmering white against the gold.

'Look at the book...look at the book...look...'

The letters shifted, twisted, turned, the gold dissolving into the white, rainbowed colours appearing around the edges of the pages, the pages themselves melting, dissolving...until Faolan suddenly found himself looking at a picture, a vague formless image, white against white, like a snowstorm. Something cold touched his face, and he felt his hair beginning to shift in the wind coming off the pages of the book.

'Put your hands flat on the book.' Lugh's voice sounded as if it was coming from very far away.

Faolan lifted his hands. They felt like lead and he could barely move them.

'Put your hands flat on the book.'

Gritting his teeth with the effort, Faolan lifted his hands. He could feel the cold sweat trickling down his face. He brought both hands over the pages and gently lowered them, palm down-wards, onto the book.

His hands went through the pages!

Faolan opened his mouth to scream...but suddenly the air was sucked from his lungs, and he was pulled forward...forward and down, down, down...into the Book of the Wind.

*

Cichal decided he would give the human-kind one chance to give up the boy and the book. Even if they gave him up he was still determined to burn the village to the ground, but he might command his Troop to be merciful. He just hadn't worked out how he was going to attack the village. The nathair couldn't be ridden over water, and the nathair master had informed him that they couldn't be taken too high into the sky, because neither Fomor nor nathair could survive the thin and cold air. So it would have to be a direct assault on the village. But there were problems with that too: the Fomor couldn't swim across because the water was too cold. The only choice open to them was to lay down a bridge. It would mean they'd be under fire from the villagers, and he doubted that these primitive human-kind were good shots.

However, he'd give them a chance to do it the easy way first.

He'd thrown the Parley Spear himself — it was a compliment to them, if only they knew. He'd been expecting some village headman to shout back a response, so he'd been surprised when the arrow with the yellow ribbon had struck deep into the ground by his feet. He'd been even more surprised when the young hook-handed bard swung out over the wall and dropped down into a little boat that bobbed in the icy water.

Cichal stepped closer to the water's edge and watched the boat come closer. The Fomor respected this human; he was clever, all bards were clever, they had to be, and Cichal wasn't particularly fond of them. They liked to think they were a special class, while in fact, they were little more than jumped-up story-tellers. There were rumours that the Emperor was thinking of curbing their powers, and the sooner the better in his opinion.

This one was different though. What was his name: Parder, Partner, Paydirt, Paedur...yes, that was it, Paedur. Cichal suspected that this young bard had taken control of the group. Certainly he had helped Faolan escape Baddalaur, and the Fomor was determined that the human would pay for that some day. He touched the knife on his belt. Someday he'd eat this human: it was the highest compliment he could pay him.

Paedur paddled the boat right into the shore. A thin coating of ice covered the water, and he could see the sliver-eels darting and twisting just beneath the surface. Twice the tiny creatures had actually attacked his paddle, burrowing small holes in the wood. He hopped out of the boat onto the hardened mud by the side of the lake and turned to face the one-eyed Fomor who had been waiting for him.

'*Deagit*,' Paedur said bowing deeply, using the ancient form of the language that the Fomor spoke amongst themselves.

Caught by surprise, Cichal bowed also. '*Deagit*,' he muttered. The serpent's forked tongue flickered, tasting the air. Usually he could tell when humans feared him; he could taste their sweaty dread on the air, but this human was different. He smelt of sweat and salt, food, turf smoke and icy water. But there was no stink of fear off him. The serpent's flat yellow eye closed, the skin drawing back off his teeth in what looked like a smile.

The young bard walked right up to the Fomor and looked up into the creature's serpent-like face. Cichal was more than twice Paedur's height, and bulky with thick powerful muscles. His heavy wood and leather armour made him seem even larger. A heavy fur-lined cloak had been thrown across his shoulders.

'You wanted to talk,' Paedur said simply.

The Fomor indicated the warriors gathered behind him with a wave of his paw. 'The village is surrounded. Give us the boy and the book, and I give you my word that I will give you all a merciful death.'

'And the alternative?'

Cichal shrugged, the pale morning light running off his eye patch. 'Then I will burn the village and slay the humans I find inside. My Troop will feast for days on their flesh.'

'I think the villagers might have something to say about that,' Paedur smiled.

'They are human-kind,' Cichal said, dismissing them with a gesture. 'We are Fomor.'

'These are not soft city humans,' Paedur said slowly, determined to keep the conversation going as long as possible. 'These are a proud people. Hunters, trappers, fishers, craftsmen. This is their village: they will fight to defend it.'

'Then they will die,' Cichal said.

'You will lose some of your Troop...and the Emperor would not like that,' Paedur added with a grin. 'What would he say if he knew you had lost Fomors to mere humans?'

Cichal's long-nailed claw shot out, but the bard's hook was faster, and Cichal found himself holding the edge of a razor-sharp half circle that took the place of the bard's left hand. The metal cut into his hard flesh, and pale pink blood oozed from the cuts. The Fomor hissed with pain and surprise. Surprisingly, he smiled again, his tongue flickering at his cut flesh. 'It will be an honour to eat you,' he announced.

The bard bowed. 'I am proud that you think so much of me. However, I'm not sure I want to be eaten,' he added.

Cichal raised his head and looked across the water to the village. 'You could have a great future in the Emperor's court,' he said very quietly. 'I could tell him that you assisted me in returning the book; he would reward you highly, probably even offer you a place in the court. For someone so young to be recognised by the Emperor would mean that you would quickly make your fortune as the human-kind and beasts in the court came to you for advice.'

'And what would I have to do for you first?' Paedur asked.

The Fomor's smile broadened; he had always known that the human-kind had no honour. 'Go back to the village and let down the bridge.'

Paedur turned to look at the village to hide the smile that crossed his face. Every moment he delayed with Cichal was valuable time for Megan, Ally and Faolan. When he turned back to the Fomor Officer, his face was expressionless. 'I'm sorry,

I'm not sure I can do that.'

It took a moment for Paedur's words to sink in, and then, in a move that was almost too fast to see, the Fomor dragged his enormous stone sword free. 'Then you won't be returning to your friends,' Cichal hissed, swinging the sword down in a deadly slashing move.

Paedur caught the blow on his hook. Sparks flew where the stone struck the metal but the force of the blow was enough to send the young bard stumbling backwards. His boots slid on the icy mud and he crashed to the ground.

Cichal reversed his two-handed grip on the sword, so that the blade pointed downwards...and then plunged forwards. Paedur twisted and the long stone blade sunk deep into the hard mud.

Cichal yanked the sword free and was lunging for the bard again, when the young man suddenly flew backwards into the icy water. The Fomor watched in amazement as he skipped and bounced on his back across the water and ice. It was only when he looked at the village that he realised the Torc Allta was hauling him back by a rope. The Fomor grabbed a spear and flung it at Ragallach. It fell short and embedded itself in the wooden fence. The second spear flew directly towards the Torc Allta, but Ragallach's enormous hand snapped out and caught the long spear in mid-air. With a quick flip of his wrist, he flung it back towards Cichal. The Fomor hissed angrily as the spear came dangerously close to hitting him. The huge beast ground his teeth in frustration. Once again the human-kind had outwitted him. Maybe he was losing his touch, maybe it was time he retired. He watched as the Torc Allta hauled the dripping youth up out of the water. At the very least he hoped some of the sliver eels had bitten him...or that he'd get a cold from the wetting. But somehow he doubted it.

'T-t-t-that-t-t-t was-s-s-s not-t-t-t mymymymy best-t-t-t idea.'
The bard's teeth were chattering so loudly he was sure some of
them were going to break. He was crouched, shivering, in the
only stone hut in the centre of the village. A fire was kept burning
here all year around. Not only did it provide a constant flame for
the villagers to light their fires from, but they believed that it was
a way of ensuring that the gods kept their eyes on the village. It
was also the warmest spot on the island, and the thick stones and
turf floor and roof ensured that it retained the heat. There was a
heavy blanket wrapped around the bard's shoulders and he was
sipping an indescribably foul drink that one of the villagers had
given him.

'It's lucky Ragallach is so strong. He hauled you back so fast
that the sliver eels didn't even get close,' Ken said.

'I know,' Paedur smiled at the Torc Allta. 'I have the bruises
to show for it.'

'What happens now?' Ken added. He was drying the bard's
clothes before the huge fire.

Paedur shrugged. 'We wait. How soon will Megan and Ally
have their potion ready?'

'I don't know,' Ken admitted, 'they won't allow me into the
hut.'

'Anything from Faolan and Lugh?'

'Nothing. Well, nothing except for the sounds...'

Paedur looked up, the firelight dancing on his face, highlighting his cheekbones and deep-sunk eyes, giving his head a curiously skull-like appearance, turning his eyes bright red. 'What sort of sounds?' he asked.

'Like wind,' Ken whispered.

*

Faolan was falling, falling, falling.

There was wind all around him. Wind in his hair, blowing it back off his face, stinging his eyes, his lips, his throat. His clothes were pressed tightly to his body, and he could feel his fingers and toes beginning to grow numb with the cold air.

He felt as if he were falling through clouds.

There were sounds all around him. The sound of wind howling, sighing, calling, keening. The wind grew louder, more insistent, pressing on him, whispering to him. There were voices in the wind, cold, chill voices. Ancient voices.

The voices whispered secrets, told tales, murmured magics. They spoke of the Great Gods, of the First Age of Man, of the Birth of Magic. A woman's voice told him the secret of the storm, a man's voice instructed how to control the air, to shape it into a physical thing. Children's voices chanted a song of the gale, telling him about the different types of breezes and how to use them.

The voices grew louder, louder, louder.

Faolan pressed his hands to his head, attempting to cover his ears. But it was no use. The words, the voices were pressing in on him. He felt as if his head was about to burst, to explode. It was too much. He was learning too much, too quickly!

There was one voice though, that was different to the others. A man's voice, harsher than the wind-voices, stronger, more insistent. Familiar. Faolan looked for this voice amongst all the others, listened for it, listening to it. Following it. Concentrating on it, he began to make out a word, a single word...'*Faolanfaolanfaolan...*' There was something about that word. With a start he realised that it was his own name. And then he realised that it was his uncle calling him. Faolan followed the voice, tracing it through the babbling voices that surrounded him. He felt as if he was rising upwards, like a swimmer coming up for air.

'Faolan!'

Faolan opened his eyes and raised his head. His golden hair shifted as if blown by a breeze, but there were no draughts in the room. The boy's nostrils flared as he tested the air, identifying the wind-carried scents, seeing the village clearly now in his mind's eye, able to place every single person by their individual odour. The wind told him a story of leather and metal, of Fomor straining as they pulled back heavy weights.

Faolan looked at his uncle as if seeing him for the first time. When he spoke, his voice was different. There was power in it; even its tone had altered, it had become deeper, like a distant rolling wind.

'The Fomor are about to fire on the village,' he said. 'Get everyone away from the walls.'

*

The air was split by a sudden scream as one hundred Fomor loosed arrows at the village. The long metal-headed shafts struck the wall around the gate. Most of the arrows stuck in the wooden wall, the metal heads biting deep into the wood, some punching through.

'They're trying to bring the bridge down,' Ragallach shouted.

Another flight of arrows screamed and whistled across the lake, all of them striking around the same spot. More wood was chipped away, enlarging the holes created by the first volley, and one of the clips holding the bridge to the wall was shot away. An arrow actually struck one of the thick cords that was used to haul up the bridge, slicing through several of the strands of rope, but not severing it.

Paedur and Ken came running up the ladder to join the Torc Allta on the wall. The pale-faced and shivering bard was still pulling on his clothes. Ragallach turned towards them, dragging them both to the ground, covering their bodies with his own as a third flight of arrows bit into the wood, continuing the destruction of the wall. Three arrows in quick succession struck the already weakened rope that held up the bridge. The final shot snapped it entirely, and the bridge shifted away from the wall, hanging forward at an awkward angle.

By now the villagers were returning fire, but their own bows were nowhere near as powerful as the Fomors' and most of the arrows fell short or bounced harmlessly off the beasts' armour.

Ally and Megan joined Ragallach, Paedur and Ken. The two young women were holding two large stone bottles. 'Sleeping honey in powder form,' Megan said, popping her head up to look over the wall. She squeaked with surprise as Ragallach dragged her back.

'It's triple strength, so it should knock out the Fomor,' Ally added. 'If only we had some way to blow it over them.'

She looked at Paedur. 'Could you conjure us up a wind?'

The bard shook his head. 'I could call up a wind, but it would simply blow the dust away. To be able to direct the wind like that takes a very special skill.' He smiled ruefully. 'I think you'd need to be a Windlord.'

A sudden warm breeze wrapped itself around them, making them turn with surprise. Faolan was standing at the foot of the ladder, looking up, his face expressionless. Spreading both hands wide, his hair was suddenly blown upwards...and then Faolan was lifted off the ground and rose up in the air. When he was level with his companions, he smiled broadly and stepped out of the empty air onto the wooden walkway.

'Now you have a Windlord,' he said simply.

'Faolan. Faolan. Human-kind.'

Cichal's voice rang out sharp and clear in the silence that followed the screaming flights of arrows. 'Listen to me, human-kind.'

'Stay down,' Paedur commanded as Faolan looked over the edge.

'They want me alive,' the young Windlord said calmly, standing up.

'I have a message for you, Faolan, from the Emperor himself,' Cichal continued.

Ragallach rose to his full height. 'Speak your message,' he boomed.

The Fomor strode down to the water's edge. Leaning on his huge sword he stared at the island fortress. 'My message is for Faolan.'

'I am here.' Faolan stood beside Ragallach. He was quite calm; he knew all he had to do was say the word and he could call up a wind that would blow the Fomor Troop away.

'Balor, Emperor of the De Danann Isle, has instructed me to say that he knows you are in possession of the Book of the Wind. You must give it up immediately.' There was a pause, as if Cichal was waiting for an answer, but when he got none, he continued. 'You should remember that the Emperor is the rightful owner of all men and goods within the De Danann Isle, and as such he is only asking for what is his.'

Ragallach snorted rudely.

'So give up the book, human-kind.'

'No,' Faolan said simply, his voice carrying on the still air.

Cichal hissed in frustration.

'Then you should know, human-kind, that when the sun rises over Falias in the morning your parents and sister will be executed as an example to those who would defy the Emperor!'

'You lie!' Faolan shouted.

'I have no need to lie,' the Fomor said simply.

'I believe him,' Paedur said.

Faolan looked at the bard, his eyes wide and troubled. 'What am I going to do? I cannot give up the book.'

'If we fly through the night, we might make it to the capital by dawn,' Paedur mused, 'but we'll need to steal at least three nathair to carry us all there.' His lips turned in a wry smile. 'All we have to do is to dispose of the Fomor first.'

Ken turned to Paedur. 'Could we not use the sleeping-honey to send them all to sleep, and then steal one of the flying serpents?'

Paedur considered for a moment before nodding. 'We can try it.' He looked at Ally and Megan. 'Open the jars.' He turned to Faolan. 'Have you mastered enough Windlore to send this dust here out over the Fomor?'

Faolan looked at the two stone jars and then at the army gathered across the lake. 'I'm sure I can,' he smiled. Stretching out his right hand, he waved it over both jars, moving it around and around in a circular motion.

For a single moment nothing happened and then, suddenly, the grey-green granules which Megan and Ally had prepared rose up out of both jars in two slowly swirling circles. The two circles joined together into a thick fuzzy spinning ball in the air above the jars. Drawing his arm back, like someone preparing to throw a stone, Faolan launched the ball at the Fomor.

The spinning green-black ball flew across the icy waters of the lake, propelled by a gently scented breeze. Instead of falling, as a normal object should, it continued in a straight line until it was positioned directly above the Fomor camp. It hung there for a single pounding heartbeat, while the beasts looked up at it...and then it exploded. Fine grey-green dust rained down on the beasts.

Tongues flickered as they tasted the air.

One of the Fomor — a huge creature, with an ugly scar across its snout — suddenly crashed to the ground. Its rasping snores sounded like wood being sawn. One by one the Fomor went down. Some attempted to run, but the triple strength sleeping-honey had already taken hold of them. Only Cichal managed to hold out long enough to fit an arrow to his bow and fire it at the figure of Faolan standing on the ramparts before he too sank into a deep slumber. The single arrow screamed its way towards Faolan's chest — until the bard's hook shot out, snapping it in two!

'Thank you,' Faolan murmured.

Paedur caught Faolan's jaw in his right hand and he turned the boy's head to stare deep into his eyes. The bard frowned. 'How much of the Windlore have you learned?' he asked.

Faolan smiled. 'All of it,' he replied, turning away. 'Shall we go and find some nathair?'

Lugh was waiting at the bottom of the steps. Faolan's uncle looked older than when they'd first met him and there were now strands of silver in his golden hair. He drew Paedur to one side and waited until the rest of the company had passed by. 'He has absorbed all the Windlore...but he doesn't understand it yet. He will *know* how to use it, but he mightn't necessarily understand how to control it. That will come with time. He must be trained to be aware of his own emotions when he's using the Windlore. He might attempt to call up a gentle breeze, but if he were angry at the time, then it might turn into a raging storm.' Lugh looked after the boy, and his golden eyes misted over with unshed tears. 'If anything happens to his parents then he will need someone to instruct him, to teach him control.'

Paedur squeezed Lugh's arm gently. 'I will look after him,' he promised.

Lugh nodded, satisfied. 'Where are you going now?'

'We'll take three nathair and ride to the capital. Maybe we can rescue Faolan's parents.'

'Beware Balor,' Lugh warned. 'He is powerful indeed.'

'Will you come with us?'

Lugh shook his head. 'I'd be of no use to you. When I was stripped of my powers, I was forbidden ever to take up arms again except in self-defence. I'm sorry.'

'Don't be,' Paedur said, 'you've made Faolan a Windlord.'

'I didn't make him,' Lugh smiled. 'He was a Windlord from the day he was born. All I did was to make him aware of it.'

The bard smiled. He nodded towards the open gate. 'Come with us. Help us choose three strong nathair to carry us south to Falias.'

Lugh grinned. 'Do you know, I used to breed nathair...oh, a long time ago. People said that they couldn't be bred in captivity, but I proved them wrong...'

Paedur and Lugh walked slowly across the bridge that had been lowered back into position. The Fomor arrows had cut away huge chunks of wood and water was seeping in through the holes. Carpenters were already beginning to work on repairing the damage, their hands wrapped in oiled leather gloves to protect them from the icy waters.

Ragallach had stopped the others from advancing onto the shore until the bard had joined them. Paedur asked Megan to ensure that all the Fomor were sleeping. The Warrior-Maid moved carefully through the piled bodies, stopping every now and again to examine them, though being very careful not to allow any of the green-black dust to touch her skin. She held a damp cloth across her face to prevent her breathing it in. She finally raised her hand.

'All clear,' Ragallach said, 'but be careful. Keep the cloths to your faces. Touch nothing.'

Ally patted the Torc Allta's hairy arm as she passed. 'You fuss too much.'

'Someone has to,' he snorted.

The companions moved through the sleeping beasts. Most of them were snorting and snoring, some twitching as if they were troubled by nightmares.

The companions found the nathair in a field behind the sleeping Fomor. Each beast had been tied to a stake driven deep into the ground, well away from the other flying serpents. Their skins were speckled with the green-black sleeping-honey dust.

They were also all asleep.

'What are we going to do now?' Faolan asked, his voice tightly controlled. He looked up into the sky. Already some of the night stars were beginning to sparkle in the cloudless skies as daylight began to fade. 'We'll never reach Falias now. Balor will execute my parents and sister with the dawn...and there's nothing I can do to stop it.'

'What am I going to do?' There were tears sparkling in Faolan's eyes as he looked at the field of sleeping nathair. The wan sunlight ran off their scales, making bright patches of rainbowed light against the dark trampled snow.

'Some of the sleeping-honey must have blown over,' Megan said quietly, looking at the light covering of dust over the flying serpents. 'They must be very sensitive to it.'

'I don't care,' Faolan said through gritted teeth, rounding on Megan. 'Because of your stupidity my parents and sister will die.' A chill breeze suddenly blew up around him, making his golden hair twist and curl around his face.

Paedur rested his hook on Faolan's arm. The touch of the icy metal startled the young man, distracting him from Megan. 'It is not the Warrior Maid's fault,' Paedur said evenly, staring deep into Faolan's eyes. 'She has saved our lives in the past with the sleeping-honey and now she has saved not only our lives but the lives of these villagers. You should be thankful to her.'

'But the nathair...' Faolan began.

'An accident. We did not know how sensitive the creatures were to the dust. And,' he added with just a touch of a smile, '*you* were controlling the wind.'

Faolan opened his mouth to reply, but closed it suddenly. He turned to Megan and apologised. 'I'm sorry. I shouldn't have spoken to you that way. I didn't know what I was saying.'

'I know you're troubled,' Megan said. 'But perhaps some of the nathair aren't sleeping deeply. We might be able to waken one.'

'Why bother?' Lugh asked.

They all turned to look at him.

'Why bother?' he repeated. 'Faolan is a Windlord now. Perhaps he does not understand all his powers, but he can control the air, he can shape the wind to his will. With such magic, nothing is impossible.' He was about to turn away, when he added, 'I was a Windrider.'

They stood in silence and watched the golden-haired man walk slowly back across the battered bridge, and then Ken asked, 'What did he mean?'

Faolan shook his head slowly. 'I'm not sure.'

'Think about it,' Paedur urged him. 'The answer lies deep in your own memories. What did your uncle say...'He was a Windrider?' Paedur looked intently at Faolan. 'He rode the wind.'

'To ride the wind,' Faolan murmured.

'What's Faolan supposed to do?' Ken asked, 'create a nathair out of thin air?'

'The air is not so thin,' Paedur murmured, 'and he doesn't have to create a nathair.' He paused and added with a smile, 'He can make anything he wishes.'

'A wind-dragon,' Faolan whispered. He looked at the bard. 'Is that what Lugh meant?'

'I think so.' Paedur looked at the five companions. 'Once in every generation there is a Windrider, a magician capable of harnessing the magic of the air. Lugh was the Windrider of his generation; you will be the Windrider for ours. Each of the Windriders traditionally creates their own beast. In the past there have been nathairs and dragons, giant butterflies, horse-like creatures with enormous wings, enormous birds.'

'Do you mean I could create an object out of thin air that would carry us south to Falias?' Faolan demanded.

'Yes,' Paedur said simply, 'if you wanted to. If you desperately *wanted* to, then yes, you could shape the wind. Do you?' he asked.

'Of course I do.'

'Then do it.'

*

Faolan stood alone in the middle of an icy field. The sun was sinking into the west behind him, throwing his long narrow shadow across the blue-white snow.

Paedur sat cross-legged on the ground closest to the young man, while Ken, Ally and Megan stood watching from a distance. Ragallach was sitting with his back to a boulder, knowing he would soon resume his boar-shape.

'What will happen?' Ken asked.

Megan shook her head. 'I don't know. I always thought that the Windriders were nothing but legends.' She looked curiously at Ally. 'Are there such things in your time?'

The young woman shrugged. 'We have nothing like this...but we have things which might seem like magic to you: flying machines, horseless carriages, boxes which carry pictures, others which carry sounds from one end of the country to the other, or from one side of the world to the other.'

'We have these things in this world too,' Megan said simply. 'I've seen all these things; they're called magic.' She nodded at Faolan. 'But I've never seen anything like that!'

In the middle of the field, the wind was gathering around Faolan. It was invisible and silent, but they could all feel its power, they could all taste the metallic sharpness in the air, smell the gathering power.

The snow beneath Faolan's feet began to shift, to twist and turn and move of its own accord. Singly and then in clumps, flakes of snow and ice rose up around his feet, spinning clockwise. The spinning circle thickened as more and more snow was sucked into it. Faolan raised his hands high above his head, drawing the circle of snow higher and higher, up to the level of his knees, to his waist, then to his chest. His eyes were closed and his head was thrown back, his golden hair tossed and blown by a breeze no-one else felt.

Clouds were racing in across the sky towards the boy, pulled by the wind. They gathered high overhead, a dark swirling mass in an otherwise clear sky. Shapes appeared in the clouds — birds, animals, creatures from myth and legend — as the clouds twisted, tumbled and coiled. In the distance thunder rumbled and the clouds were briefly highlighted as lightning crackled.

The spinning column of snow completely encircled Faolan. The funnel rose upwards, sucking the snow and ice from the ground, funnelling it upwards into the clouds, exposing rock that had been covered for generations.

The mass of cloud began to drift lower. It was now joined to the ground by the funnel of swirling snow that swept around the boy. The cloud was in constant motion. It had darkened to a sullen, almost metallic grey that was occasionally shot through with silver or stark white as lightning flared deep within it. The air tasted flat and sharp, vaguely unpleasant, and the companions were all aware that the hair on their heads and necks and the back of their hands was standing on end.

'What is it?' Ally breathed, trying to make sense of the shape that was forming before their eyes.

Megan shook her head. 'A bird perhaps?'

Paedur scrambled to his feet and backed away from the mass of cloud that was now hovering just off the ground. There was no sign of Faolan who was lost somewhere deep within it.

'It's a dragon,' Ken said, eyes wide with wonder.

The cloud continued to twist and shape and re-shape itself, but it was assuming a dragon-like shape. A huge grey-white creature of cloud and wind, snow and ice. A long narrow head appeared, eyes wide and flat, like polished ice, then a slender neck, followed by an enormous body with ribbed bat-like wings. It was almost painful to look at the creature, because of the way the cloud body kept shifting. It turned its head and opened its mouth, and icy wind wafted over the companions. Its teeth were slivers of ice.

And then Faolan appeared.

He was standing on the back of the wind-dragon, and the cloud which had created the magical creature had wrapped itself around him in a shining metallic-looking armour. When he spoke his voice echoed slightly, booming like the wind.

'I am Faolan the Windlord. Ride with me to Falias.'

One by one the companions approached the wind-dragon. Its flesh felt cold, though soft to their touch.

Paedur climbed up first and then hauled Ally and Megan up beside him. Ken and Ragallach followed, though as the Torc Allta settled himself onto the magical creature's back, the last of the daylight faded and he transformed into his were-beast shape.

'Balor will learn to fear the Windlords,' Faolan said, his eyes wide and wild as the wind-dragon rose upwards over the sleeping nathair and Fomor.

'Don't underestimate the Emperor,' Paedur warned. 'You will never meet a more powerful magician.'

'I control the wind,' Faolan cried aloud.

'No-one ever truly controls the wind. You can command it, but commanding it and controlling it are two different things.'

'I am the Windrider.'

Far below, the island village was nothing more than a dozen scattered lights. None of the companions saw Lugh standing by the gate watching the elegant wind-dragon rise gracefully into the darkening sky. None of them saw the tears on his face. Seeing Faolan ride the wind reminded him of his own youth and the days when he too had been a Windlord.

He hoped Faolan used the power wisely. If he didn't, it would destroy him.

*

Far to the south, in the heart of Falias, the capital of the De Danann Isle, a single ruby-red light burned in the palace's highest towers. In a small circular room at the top of the tower, a figure, half-man, half-Fomor was hunched over a bowl of silver liquid. The shifting blood-red light made his metallic half-mask seem alive.

Balor of the Evil Eye smiled broadly, revealing his triangular razor-sharp Fomor teeth. The boy was coming. He had seen him riding the wind.

So Faolan had learned a little of the Windlore. No matter. He would be no match for Balor's dark magics. When Balor had finished with him, he would tell the secrets of the Windlore. And then Balor would rule the known world. The Emperor threw back his head and laughed his hissing, rasping laugh.

At the foot of the stairs leading up to the tower, the Fomor guards, who feared nothing and no-one, shivered at the sound.

The crowds had begun to arrive long before the dawn.

The Emperor himself had decreed that everyone should attend the execution of the wizards who called themselves the Lords of the Wind.

And no-one even thought about staying away: it was unwise to upset the Emperor.

Few people there knew the Windlords. Some were aware of the legends surrounding the magicians, they knew they controlled the wind, ensured that there were good harvests and kept the storms away from the De Danann Isle. They seemed to work for good; there didn't seem to be any reason to execute them...but the Emperor obviously had his reasons, and no-one was prepared to question those.

There was an almost carnival atmosphere in the city. A public holiday had been declared. People had come in from the surrounding countryside, and humans, beasts and were-folk mingled together. Flags and bunting hung from most of the houses and shops, and the streets were lined with stalls, selling everything from food to jewellery. Jugglers and circus performers acted on street corners, while singers and musicians chose corners that echoed and amplified their voices.

A stranger to the city might well have thought there was something to celebrate, but one only had to listen carefully to realise that the laughter was too loud, it was too strained, and just a little too forced. Some of the songs were slightly off key, the jugglers dropped their balls and sticks more frequently than they should, and the magician's tricks went wrong far too often.

And the stranger to Falias might have realised that there seemed to be far too many troops moving through the city. They were mostly humans moving in pairs and groups of four, but some of the Emperor's own Fomor were also visible, the huge beasts towering above even the tallest humans.

In the deepest dungeon in Balor's castle, Cian and Etain, Faolan's father and mother, and Grannia, his sister, waited. Cian had recovered a little from the effects of the magic he had worked in Baddalaur, but he was still terribly weak. And because they were so far below the earth where the air was stale and the wind never blew, they were unable to use any of their magic.

They had remained awake through the night, not talking, sitting huddled together, taking comfort from each other's presence, knowing they were going to be executed with the coming of dawn. The only light in the dungeon was a tiny stump of a candle that gave off a foul smell. Watching it burn lower and lower, they knew that dawn was approaching.

As the candle at last guttered out, Grannia asked, 'Did Faolan escape?'

'I'm sure he did,' Cian said softly, his voice little more than a whisper.

'Balor would have told us if he'd captured your brother,' Etain said quietly. 'He likes to boast.'

'I wonder where he is now?' Grannia whispered.

'Far away from here,' Etain said confidently.

*

It had been impossible to sleep on the terrifying high-speed flight into the south. The dragon flew like the wind and Ally wasn't sure whether the howling she heard was coming from the creature or was just the sound of the air gusting by. No-one spoke because speech was impossible and everyone concentrated on hanging onto a creature whose flesh was soft and silky one moment, hard and slippery the next. Ragallach, now in his were-beast shape as a boar, huddled close to Ally and she was glad of the warmth the hairy pig gave off. Faolan stood close to the head of the creature, controlling it with reins that sparkled and glittered like ice.

Ken saw the city first. He felt his heart begin to pound with shock and surprise and, catching his sister's eye, he pointed straight ahead. Ally looked, and he saw her eyes widen with shock.

Ken and Ally had seen Baddalaur, and some of the smaller villages in the Northlands. They had been expecting Falias to be something similar. Instead, they found they were approaching an enormous modern-looking city, with buildings soaring eight and nine stories in the sky, intersected with straight regular roads, rectangular parklands, circular pools and lakes, broad plazas and elegant squares. But it wasn't its sheer size which took their breath away: it was the roofs of the buildings. All the buildings in Falias, from the smallest to the largest, were roofed in gold. In the pale pre-dawn light the city shimmered and sparkled and both children could only guess what it would look like when the sun hit it.

'Falias,' Paedur shouted back, 'the City of Gold. Each of the four cities of the De Danann grew up around mining villages. Falias was the largest and because it mined gold, it became the wealthiest. The others mined silver, iron and tin.'

Faolan glanced back over his shoulder. 'Where's the main square?' he called.

The bard pointed down. 'Just follow the crowds.'

*

In his high tower in the centre of the city, Balor turned away from the narrow slit window. They were coming. He had seen the grey cloud on the horizon and known immediately by the disturbance in the atmosphere that the cloud was magical. He would allow the boy to come closer and then he would strike him down. Soon...soon...soon, the secret of the Windlore would be his!

Faolan brought the wind-dragon to a stop over one of the tall buildings. 'Everyone off,' he said quickly, looking at the horizon. The sun was just about to rise.

Ken slid down onto the roof and helped his sister down. She had Ragallach tucked under one arm. Megan ignored his hand and jumped easily to the ground. Paedur and Faolan argued for a moment and then the bard jumped down. As soon as he touched the ground, the wind-dragon rose back up into the sky.

'What's happening?' Ken demanded.

Paedur shrugged. 'This is something he has to do by himself.'

'We must help,' Megan said quietly.

Paedur smiled. 'We will help.'

As he spoke the sun touched the horizon, sending long shafts of morning sunlight across the pale purple sky. The boar jumped out of Ally's arms and wriggled and writhed on the ground, assuming its man-like shape in a matter of moments. The huge beast rose to its feet and pointed to where the cloud was descending over a square a few streets away. 'He may be a Windlord,' he snuffled, 'but he still needs our help.'

Paedur looked at Ken and Ally. 'You are not of this world. This is not your fight, you should stay here.'

Ally glanced at her brother. 'We've come this far, we won't back out now.'

'There will be fighting, and neither of you have been trained to fight.'

'We want to help,' Ally said, looking directly at the bard.

'If you are injured, you will carry that injury with you back to your own world. If you are killed, even Faolan with all his wind magic will not be able to bring you back to life again.'

'We're wasting time,' Ken said bravely, although his heart was pounding madly in his chest. 'Let's go.'

Faolan's parents and sister had been brought up out of the dungeon. With their hands in chains, they had been marched out into the square that faced the palace and made to stand at the foot of the steps.

A hush fell over the crowd, radiating outwards from those nearest the prisoners. The square immediately filled with people eager to see what was happening and the numbers of human and Fomor guards increased rapidly.

And then a name rippled through the crowd, and suddenly the people seemed far more nervous, no longer quite so eager to be at the front of the crowd. 'Balor,' they whispered, 'Balor. Balor is coming. The Emperor is coming.'

It was as if the entire city had fallen silent, and now held its breath, waiting.

The palace doors swung silently open.

Balor's palace had been built in the centre of Falias. It was a tall, spectacular-looking building even by De Danann standards, completely circular with enormous arched windows that rose up from the ground and flooded the interior with light. The doors were of a peculiar dark wood that had been carved and etched with scenes from De Danann history. The entire building had been covered with a thin gold foil. It had been Balor's intention to have the building constructed of gold, but the metal had proven too soft to carry the weight of the roof while the golden doors had been too heavy and had ripped away from their hinges. When the rising sun struck the building it blazed with light, making it almost difficult to look upon, and in the evenings it burned blood-red with the spectacular sunsets.

Cian squinted into the light. He had seen the shadow appear in the golden wall of light and knew that the doors were opening, but it was hard to be sure.

'Balor's coming,' Grannia whispered, and he was proud that he heard no fear in his daughter's voice.

Turning his head slightly, Cian discovered that he could make out some detail.

'It's the Emperor,' Etain murmured quietly.

A figure appeared out of the shimmering light. The shape was unmistakably human...but it was immediately evident that there was something wrong with it. The figure was taller than any normal human and it was broader, the arms unnaturally long, the head slightly misshapen, the thick black hair greasy with a faintly greenish tinge to it. But what immediately caught everybody's attention was the shining metal mask that covered the left side of the Emperor's face. The mask had been shaped to match the right side of his face, but no-one had ever seen what lay beneath the mask...and lived.

Balor strode down the steps and stopped before the Wind-lords. Placing both hands on his hips, he glared at them. Grannia noticed that his nails were unnaturally long and pointed. She knew that Balor's father had been a Fomor, his mother a human, and the girl had heard the story that he had been born with a Fomor-like tail.

'Windlords, this is your final chance.' His voice was a rasping hiss. 'Give me the secret of the Wind.'

'Impossible,' Cian said proudly.

'Nothing is impossible,' Balor hissed. 'Give me the secret or I will slay you now and take the secret from the boy.'

'What boy?' Etain asked quickly.

'Why, none other than your son.'

'Faolan is far from here,' Etain said quickly.

Balor shook his huge head and ran his fingers through his hair, pulling it back off his face. 'Not so. My Fomor chased your boy into the Northlands. He made his way to his uncle's village. Maybe he was hoping that Lugh the Windrider would come to your rescue, so he obviously didn't know that the Windrider had been stripped of his powers a long time ago.'

'Because of you,' Cian snapped.

'Perhaps. But that was then and this is now. Lugh seems to have instructed the boy in the Windlore...or at least enough of it to allow him to conjure a wind-dragon. Aaah,' Balor hissed delightedly, 'I can see that you're surprised. So, you will be even more surprised to discover that he has come for you. Look!'

The Emperor jabbed a taloned hand into the air. The clouds over Falias suddenly twisted and coiled together...and then the wind-dragon appeared over the roofs of the houses trailing tendrils of grey-white cloud. The figure of Faolan standing on its back seemed very small indeed. The magical creature's enormous wings flapped slowly sending wind gusting through the crowded streets. The wind-dragon opened its long narrow mouth and howled like a rising storm.

The wind-dragon dropped lower, and now wind from the beating of its enormous wings was strong enough to knock people to the ground. Even the huge Fomor staggered in the strong gusts.

'I have come for my family.' Faolan's voice sounded like the howling of the wind.

Balor threw back his head and laughed.

The wind-dragon moved even lower over the streets. Its wings scraped the sides of buildings, blowing off golden roof tiles, ripping off shutters, pulling down awnings. The people directly below the creature were tumbled along the street among bits and pieces of trash. The crowd panicked and ran.

Faolan leaned forward across the neck of the magical creature. 'Release my parents,' he boomed.

'I've been waiting for you, young Windlord,' Balor cried. 'You have fallen into my trap!' Raising both hands to his face, Balor undid the clips that held his mask in place.

'Don't look,' Cian shouted. 'Don't look into his face. Get

down,' he shouted, struggling to face his wife and daughter. 'Get down.' They both dropped to the ground, their eyes squeezed shut.

One of the Fomor guards standing behind Cian forgot to lower his gaze. The sight of Balor without his mask froze him rigid with fright, and as he continued to stare at the Emperor, Balor lifted his head to look at him. His single human eye blazed with a cold green fire and his other eye — the inhuman eye — that was normally hidden beneath the mask, glittered with an icy blue fire. The Fomor's scales lost their shimmering rainbow hue and turned the colour of old ash. The flesh stiffened with a faint crackling sound and within a dozen heartbeats the Fomor had hardened into solid stone. His companion looked at him and immediately dropped to the ground alongside the Windlords.

Balor raised his head to look at the wind-dragon.

Faolan got a brief glimpse of what lay behind the Emperor's mask before he called up a mist to shield himself from Balor's horrific face, but even that single instant had been enough to send an icy chill through his body, locking his muscles, hardening his bones. The right half of the Emperor's face was human. The left hand side was like something from a nightmare. It was neither human nor Fomor, but something in between, the skull completely bald, and the eye had the long slit-pupil of the serpent folk.

Balor's green and blue eyes blazed and a portion of the wind-dragon turned to stone and came crashing down onto the street, shattering into rubble. Faolan was thrown to one side and very nearly fell to the ground. He desperately called in more clouds to rebuild the wind-dragon. He directed a section of cloud to fall onto Balor, completely enwrapping him in a chill, damp blanket - but Balor froze the cloud to ice and shattered it with a blow of his fist.

'I am the Emperor of the De Danann Isle, the mightiest magician this world has ever known,' Balor crowed, 'and you are but a boy. You cannot hope to defeat me.' Raising both hands high, he stretched out his fingers and tiny slivers of black fire darted from them. They hissed through the wind-dragon, slicing away a portion of the body, the clawed feet, the tip of one wing, turning it to black dust where they touched. The wind-dragon's howling became a shriek, and it began to spiral down to the ground.

Drawing on his newly learned lore, Faolan called in the bitter northern wind. A flurry of snow and ice danced through Falias's broad streets and by the time it reached the steps of the palace, it was a blizzard. It gathered around the Emperor, coating him in ice, the force of the breeze sending him staggering backwards.

Balor's gaze turned the snow and ice brittle, but Faolan kept on calling up more and more wind magic, intensifying the cold around the Emperor, driving sleet into his mis-matched eyes, freezing his exposed skin, deafening him with a howling gale.

For a few moments, it looked as if it might work...and then the young Windlord realised that the wind-dragon was disintegrating. With all his efforts concentrated on the Emperor, he was unable to hold the clouds together.

The momentary confusion and lapse of concentration was enough to send him falling to the ground. The fall stunned him and as he lay there, the hail and wind that had howled around Balor died as suddenly as it had arisen. The Emperor stretched his arms wide, and a thin layer of ice fell from his rich robes. Striding forward, he stepped across the still bodies of Faolan's family and approached the young Windlord where he lay on the ground. 'I'm surprised at your powers,' Balor said quietly. 'I should be thankful that you will not live long enough to learn to use them properly. You might have become a problem if that had ever happened.'

Faolan attempted to rise to his feet, but the Emperor created a ball of fire that hung in the air just above the boy, and stung his back as he rose up.

Balor crouched down beside Faolan. 'Now, you will tell me the secret of the Windlore.'

Faolan shook his head, his eyes squeezed tightly shut. The ball of fire drifted lower, close enough to singe Faolan's leather jerkin.

'You will tell me,' Balor hissed. He crouched down beside

Faolan and caught his face in his long-nailed hands. 'I can turn you to stone, but still keep you alive,' he whispered. 'Think about that. Think about being trapped in a body of stone, unable to move, unable to do anything, but still aware. Think about that. Now, tell me the secret of the Windlore!' he demanded.

'Never,' Faolan said through gritted teeth.

Balor hissed in rage. He touched the boy's face with his long-nailed finger. 'Open your eyes, boy, look at me.'

Faolan squeezed his eyes tighter.

Balor touched Faolan's eyelid. 'Open your eyes, look at me...'

*

'What are we going to do?' Ally demanded. 'We have to do something!'

The five companions were in a house directly across the square from the palace. They had ducked into the building when the blizzard had come howling through the streets. The building obviously served as an inn, but the long tables were now deserted and the fire in the hearth had burnt low. They had a clear view of Faolan's family crouched at the foot of the steps, with a Fomor guard lying on the ground beside them. There was a statue of a second Fomor on the steps beside them, its face frozen into an expression of absolute terror. Balor was squatting on the ground beside Faolan and even from across the square they could clearly hear the Emperor's questions, and Faolan's replies.

'I can only see the one Fomor,' Megan observed. She slid a narrow-bladed throwing knife from its sheath on her belt. 'I believe I could strike it from here.'

'I believe you could,' Paedur said softly, 'but what about Faolan?'

Ragallach rubbed his paw against the bubbled glass of the house they were hiding in. 'If Megan were to throw her knife at the Fomor, I believe I could get to Balor before he realised what was happening.'

Paedur patted the Torc Allta's arm. 'And what then, my friend? You are strong indeed, far stronger than any human I know. But Balor is half Fomor; all he has to do is to throw you off and get you to look at his face...and you're stone.'

'Would these help?' Ally asked quickly, producing two small stone pots from beneath her cloak.

Paedur stared at them for a moment and then a broad smile lit up his face. 'I believe they might just do,' he said. He reached into his own pouch and removed a matching pot. 'I'd forgotten I had it.'

Ragallach squinted at the pots. 'What are they?'

'Sleeping-honey in powdered form,' Ally explained. She glanced out of the window. 'We know the effect it has on the Fomor, but what'll it do to the Emperor?'

Paedur handed one of the pots to Ragallach. He handed the second pot to Megan. 'We're about to find out,' he said slowly, rolling the small stone pot in the palm of his hand. 'Megan and I will try to drop our pots at the Emperor's feet. Ragallach, try to hit the guard.'

'Hurry,' Ken said urgently, 'Balor's making Faolan open his eyes...'

*

The three pots sailed out across the square. One struck the Fomor in the chest and shattered against the studs on his breastplate. A cloud of green-black smoke rose up around his head. The Fomor blinked in astonishment, his forked tongue tasting the air...and then crashed to the ground.

The remaining two pots landed close to Balor's left hand, smashing to pieces on the cobbles. He shouted aloud with fright — and breathed in a lungful of the thick dust! But instead of falling to his feet, Balor rose upwards, arms raised high, screaming with rage. The very air around him crackled with energy, and when he ran his fingers through his hair, it flickered and sputtered with bright sparks. His right hand shot out, pointing directly towards the inn where the companions were hiding. A fist-sized ball of yellow-white light darted towards the building, but splashed harmlessly off the exterior wall. A second ball smashed in through the glass and bounced around the room, igniting everything it touched.

'Outside,' Paedur shouted, 'outside.'

More and more of the fireballs were darting into the room now, and within seconds it had become an inferno. But as the companions rushed outside, coughing, blinking smoke and ashes from their eyes, they found they were facing an even greater hazard: the Emperor's terrible gaze.

The huge half-man was glaring at them, swaying slightly from side to side with the effects of the sleeping-honey, his eyes red-rimmed.

'What now?' Ken coughed.

'Run,' Paedur said.

'Where, which way?'

'Anywhere.'

'Too late, too late,' Balor screamed. With a quick flick of his wrist, he launched five flaming fireballs towards the humans.

Ally grabbed her brother's hand and ran. But she knew there was no way they could outrun the fireballs. She saw Paedur turn, his hook raised high...she saw Ragallach turn back for the bard...she saw Megan launch her knife towards the Emperor, saw it bounce off his chest. She saw the fireballs that were streaming towards Ken and herself. They were as big as a man's head, perfectly circular flaming balls of yellow-white fire. Even at a distance, they gave off tremendous heat. As she watched, they sped right up to her.

Ally opened her mouth and screamed because she realised she was about to die.

Ken screamed because his sister was squeezing his fingers so tightly...

*

The fireballs stopped in mid-air as if they had run into an invisible wall. The ball was so close to the bard that it actually singed his eyebrows, curling and crisping the dark hairs on his face.

There was a sound like an sudden intake of breath — and then the fireballs sped backwards towards Balor!

On the steps behind him, Faolan raised his hands, dragging the fireballs back to Balor. When Balor had turned his attention to the companions, Faolan had used the opportunity to slide free.

He had one final chance to defeat Balor. He would not fail.

The five fireballs exploded against the Emperor, wrapping him in fire, but Balor threw back his head and laughed...and the fires vanished, leaving him unmarked.

Drawing on the last of his power, Faolan called up a cyclone. A funnel of wind stretched down from the clouds and wrapped itself around Balor, swallowing him up. The whirlwind was spinning so fast that it was impossible to see what lay within. Lightning twisted and sparked within the whirling funnel of wind. Balor's laughter became a scream that the wind echoed and re-echoed across the capital.

Faolan raised his hands high, and the cyclone began to rise up off the ground. The boy brought his hands above his head, and the whirling cone of wind was sucked up into the clouds...taking Balor with it. Thunder crashed and rolled through the clouds, and the lightning that burned deep in the heart of the tunnel of wind intensified, turning the dark clouds into angry masses of fire.

Moments later a strong breeze swept across Falias, blowing away the clouds, allowing the city to be bathed in bright, warm sunlight. There was no sign of Balor.

Faolan just about managed to stagger down the steps before he collapsed into his mother's arms, exhausted by the tremendous effort.

Cian ran his hands through his son's sweat-dampened hair. 'You were a boy when you left us,' he whispered. 'I never thought you'd return to us a Windlord!'

'Are you sure this will work?' Ally asked nervously.

'I'm sure,' Faolan said lightly. He brought the wind-dragon round in a slow, spiralling turn over the college town of Baddalaur.

'But will you be able to get us back to our own time?' Ken persisted.

'I will. I am a Windlord, after all,' he added with a grin.

'You still have a lot to learn,' Paedur said quickly.

'I've got a good teacher though,' Faolan laughed. 'I think I can learn a lot from you.'

'I've still got a lot to learn myself,' Paedur murmured. He suddenly yelped with fright as the tip of the wind-dragon's wing knocked a dozen tiles off the tower's roof. 'And you've still got a lot to learn about controlling this creature.' Faolan brought the creature lower until it was above the Baddalaur marshlands. Ken touched his sister's shoulder pointing to the steps which had appeared out of the mist at their left hand side. 'Back where we started, eh?' he said.

'I never thought I'd be delighted to see those steps again,' Ally said feelingly. Faolan did something with the wind-dragon that made it change its shape so that it looked like a long narrow boat. It even rocked from side to side as Ragallach leaned over and caught the edge of the steps with his paw, pulling them in close to it. Paedur caught the other end with his hook, and together they held the cloud-boat secure while Megan helped Ally and Ken up on to the worn stone steps.

Brother and sister stood there for a moment, unwilling or unable to comprehend that their adventure was at an end. 'What's going to happen to you all?' Ally asked, trying to put off the final moment for as long as possible.

'Faolan will remain with me in Baddalaur,' Paedur answered. 'I'll try to teach him some respect for the power he now possesses. Ragallach has decided to stay here also; he will be the first of the non-human races to train as a bard. He will be able to add a whole new body of folklore and legend to our records.' Paedur turned to look at the warrior maid. 'Megan has decided that she will return to her village...in a season or two. She needs to go adventuring.'

'I think I've developed a taste for adventure,' Megan said quickly. 'Maybe I'll come this way next season, and we'll see what trouble I can get into.'

Faolan gestured with his hand, plucking at the edge of the cloud and then blowing into his clenched fist. Stretching out his hand to Ken and Ally, he handed them two small circular silver-grey pendants, each one etched with a swirling design — like frozen cloud. 'If ever you need me, or if you ever want to go adventuring again, just hold these in your fists and breathe on them.' He nodded to the steps. 'Walk on down. You'll find yourself in your own time.'

'Thank you,' Ken said.

Ally nodded. She went and sat on the steps beside Ragallach, the Torc Allta. 'Thank you,' she said simply. 'You know, before I met you, I was afraid of...people who looked different, people from different backgrounds. You've taught me that it's not just looks that matter.'

The Torc Allta grunted. 'And you taught me that not all humans are cruel or evil.'

'You never told me what you were doing the night I found you in that pit.'

Ragallach grunted. 'I had gone in search of adventure,' he laughed. 'And I found it.'

'Quickly, quickly,' Faolan urged them. 'It's going to be difficult calling up the Timewinds *and* keeping this cloud together. Start counting,' he called as the cloud drifted away from the steps. 'By the time you reach thirty you should be back in your own time.'

'And if we're not?' Ally shouted.

'Then we'll meet you at the bottom of the steps.'

*

'Sixteen...seventeen...eighteen...nineteen...Do you think the cloud is getting lighter?' Ally asked.

'I don't know, but the air certainly smells different,' her brother said, looking around and breathing deeply. 'I can smell the sea,' he added, trying to keep the excitement in his voice under control.

'Twenty-three...twenty-four...'

The cloud was almost gone now and they could hear the sea and the gulls in the air around them.

'I didn't feel anything, did you?' Ken asked. 'I thought I'd feel something when we went forward in time.'

'How do we know this is our own time?' Ally asked, a sudden thought chilling her. 'How do we know Faolan managed to send us back to exactly the right spot at the right time? Maybe this is Skellig Michael, but three hundred years in the past, or a thousand years in our future.'

'Twenty-eight...twenty-nine...'

'Thirty,' they both shouted together.

'And where have you two been? We very nearly missed the tide...' Their father, small and stout, with a bristling black moustache came towards them, smiling broadly. 'Did you have a good day?'

Ally and Ken looked at one another and laughed, their voices high and shrill with relief and surprise.

'We had a great day, Dad,' Ken said.

'Your mother was afraid you might be bored,' Robert Morand smiled, 'but I told her you'd find something to do.'

'Oh, we found one or two things that kept us amused for a while,' Ally said lightly, trying to keep a straight face.

'Good...good. Our day was a bit of a disaster though. It took us all day to get the engine fixed. So we'll have to come back here tomorrow to do our research,' he added, turning away. He stopped suddenly. 'What are you wearing?' he asked in astonishment.

They looked at one another: they were still wearing their leather jerkins, leather trousers and high boots. The clothes were soiled and scuffed.

'Were you wearing those this morning?' Robert asked suspiciously.

'Dad,' Ally said with a laugh, 'we've been wearing these for days. Haven't we, Ken?'

'Absolutely.'

Their father looked at the leather clothes again and then turned away, muttering about fashions. Ken turned to Ally and smiled. 'You know, for a moment there I thought it might have been a dream...'

Ally shook her head. She opened her hand. The circular pendant Faolan had given her glittered against her dirty flesh. Ken opened his hand. The twisting, swirling design frozen onto the face of his pendant differed slightly from his sister's.

'It wasn't a dream,' Ally said. She turned to look across the heaving grey sea to where their hired yacht bobbed at anchor. 'I feel different,' she said, glancing back at her brother. She took a deep breath, remembering the hook-handed bard, the Windlord, the Warrior Maid and the Torc Allta. She didn't expect she'd ever see them again. Though she had known them only for a few days, she had learned so much from them...they had changed her. 'I feel...older,' she said finally.

Ken nodded. He knew what she meant. Their strange, bizarre experiences had changed them both. 'Would you do it again?' he asked.

Ally tilted her head, considering. 'Yes...no. Maybe. I don't know.'

Ken brought his hand to his mouth, holding up the pendant

between thumb and forefinger. 'What did Faolan say?' he asked, his eyes twinkling mischievously. 'All we have to do is to blow on them...'

Ally turned back to snatch the pendant from her brother's hand. 'Don't even think about it,' she laughed. 'Well, not just yet anyway!'